FIND ME IN DARKNESS

DARKNESS

A DARK PLEASURES NOVELLA

MAL & CHRISTINA (PART 1)

BY JULIE KENNER

CHAPTER 1

MAL STOOD BY the bed and looked down at the woman he'd just fucked.

She was drop-dead gorgeous, lithe and strong with alabaster skin and hair as dark as his own. She was smart and funny, had good taste in wine, and had sucked his cock with rare skill.

Not a bad resume, when you got right down to it, and if Mal had even an ounce of sense he'd slide back into bed, sink deep inside her, and try once more to forget how goddamn lonely he was.

Shit.

She didn't deserve that. Hell, none of the

women he fucked deserved that. Which was why he had a strict one-time only policy. Shared lust and pounding sex to work out some of life's kinks was one thing. But Mal didn't do serious or personal. Not anymore.

He'd had serious. He'd had personal.

Hell, he'd had love. Epic, forever, every-one-else-can-just-melt-away love.

And not only love, but respect and humor and passion so intense that he felt alive only when he touched her.

He'd had all that.

Now, all he had was a nightmare.

On the bed, the woman shifted, then smiled up at him, soft and sultry. "Mal? What's wrong?"

He said nothing, and she sat up, letting the sheet fall to her waist to expose her bare breasts as she held out a hand to him. "Come back to bed and let me make it better."

If only it was that easy.

"I have to go."

"Go?" She glanced at the clock and then

pulled up the sheet to cover her nakedness. "It's not even midnight." Her voice was indignant.

"It can't be helped."

"You son-of-a-bitch."

He didn't wince, didn't try to defend himself. What defense was there against the truth?

Instead, he moved to her side, then brushed his fingers lightly over her forehead. "Sleep," he said, then stepped away as the woman fell back against the pillows, lost once again to the world of dreams.

He pulled the sheet up to cover her, then glanced around the room in search of his clothes. He'd brought her to the penthouse suite at the stunning Gardiner Hotel, a relatively new Fifth Avenue boutique in which he held a significant financial position. Now he moved through the bedroom and parlor, gathering discarded garments as he walked.

He pulled on his jeans, then slipped his arms into the white button-down that he'd worn that evening before going out in search of a woman to take the edge off. He let it hang open as he stepped out onto the patio, then moved to the stone half-wall that separated him from the concrete and asphalt of Fifth Avenue twelve stories below.

It would be easy enough to jump. To end his pain, even if only for a few moments.

And a few moments were all that he would get before the phoenix fire would surround and gather him, reducing him to ashes before once again regenerating him.

Immortality.

Had he truly once believed it was a gift? To have an eternity in this body that could touch and feel and experience such profound pleasure?

Three thousand years ago, it *had* been a gift, but that was when she'd been beside him, and it was Christina he'd been touching. Caressing.

Christina he'd held in his arms. Whose lips brushed gently over his skin. Who whispered soft words so close to his ear that even her breath aroused him.

But then everything had gone to shit and he'd realized that immortality wasn't a gift. It was a curse.

He was immortal. He was alone. And every goddamn day was torture.

He closed his eyes and clutched the railing, his hands clenched so tight that the rough-hewn edges of the stone cut into his palms.

Christina…

He reached out with his mind, searching for her as he did every night with equal parts dread and longing.

Sometimes centuries would pass before he felt her presence resonate through him, sometimes only decades.

It had been two hundred and sixty years since the last time he'd found her, her energy reaching out to him from across the Atlantic, though she never had a conscious memory of him, or even of herself.

He'd gone to her—and once more, he'd

done what he had to do.

Since then, he'd grown complacent, expecting—no, *hoping*—that he would not feel her. That he would not find her out there in the world.

That he would not have to go to her yet again.

Christina…

Nothing. Not even the slightest tingle of awareness.

Thank god.

He breathed deep, relieved, and slowly let his body relax. He turned to go back inside, but the moment he did, everything shifted. The force of her essence lashed out, catching him unaware.

It surrounded him. Burned through him.

Hot. Powerful. Desperate.

And close.

This time, she was close. So close that it wasn't just her essence that filled his mind, but *her*. The memory of her scent enveloped him, the sensation of her skin against his, the taste of her lips, of her flesh.

Oh, god. Oh, Christ.

He sank to his knees, wanting to run. Wanting to retch.

But he could do neither. And slowly—so painfully slowly—he stood.

He would do what he had to do, the same as he had done over and over again for millennia.

He would find her.

He would allow himself one moment to look at her.

And then, goddamn him, he would kill her.

CHAPTER 2

"WE SHOULD HAVE stayed in tonight."

I shoot Brayden an irritated look. "On my first night in New York? No way."

"Dammit, Jaynie, you fainted on the airplane."

"One," I say, counting out on my fingers for effect, "now that I'm in New York, I'm Christina, not Jaynie." At the ripe old age of twenty-three, I've joined the ranks of walking cliches everywhere and have moved to Manhattan to live with my rich best friend while I struggle to become an actress. Christina is the name my mom called me when she was in her gray mood. And even though it twists me up inside every time I think about my mother, I still want that stage name. But whether that's because I'm honoring my mother or punishing myself, I really don't know.

I flash him a winning smile. "Of course that's just for my adoring fans. You can stick with Jaynie."

He rolls his eyes. "Like I said, *Jaynie*, you fainted on the plane."

I ignore him and hold up another finger. "Two, I was completely checked out by the paramedics." I bite back a frown, because despite the perky no-problem attitude I'm displaying for Brayden, the whole thing really was freaky.

"Look, if you really fainted, that's one thing. I mean, it's not a great thing, but at least it's not—you know."

I do know. Throughout my entire child-hood, I suffered from episodes where I just sort of checked out. My mother's shrink—who I refuse to call *my* shrink despite having seen him on and off for years—called the episodes fugues. But I'm not sure he was right. I looked up the word when I was ten, and according to the dictionary at my elementary school, a fugue state involves a loss of identity. And although sometimes I was completely gone, other times it was like I was watching a movie. I was still *me*—I was just me watching bad shit happen. Bad shit that I could never specifically remember when I came out of it, but that left me feeling edgy and shaky.

I tried to explain that to the shrink once, but all he did was make more notes in my chart.

I tried to explain it to Brayden, too, and it just made him look worried.

After that, I stopped trying to explain it at all. I had enough problems with a suicidal mother who would fall into what she called "gray moods" that would last for weeks, and during which she would repeatedly tell me that I had the devil living inside me and that she should never have had me because I was going to destroy the world.

Honestly, is it any wonder I have self-esteem issues?

When I joined the drama club in high school and started to get cast in plays and musicals regularly, the episodes became less and less frequent. I never got a solid explanation from the shrink, who only said that I was outgrowing them, but I knew that wasn't the real reason. It was the acting. I became someone else on stage. And I think that I was becoming someone else when I checked out, too. So my theory is that the acting filled some weird *your mother is crazy and you want to be someone else* need that I've never wanted to examine too closely.

Frankly, I don't care about the reason. I love acting. And if doing something I love keeps me from going to la-la land, then as far as I'm concerned, that's just one more ticky-mark in the plus column.

Brayden is still looking at me with his concerned I'm-going-to-be-a-doctor-and-must-fix-this expression.

"I told you. I really fainted." I want him

to believe me, both because I don't want him to worry and because I want him to drop it. But I'm not entirely certain that I'm telling the truth. The incident didn't feel like one of my fugues. But at the same time, I never completely passed out, so I don't know that it was technically a faint. Instead, I felt like I was being turned inside out.

When I was eleven, I really did faint once. I'd been standing in line for hours at Six Flags Over Texas and it was hot, and I hadn't drunk any water in hours. The world had turned sort of red, then sort of gray, and then my knees couldn't seem to hold me up anymore and I just crumpled to the ground. All in all, it had been a rather non-violent experience, which I guess is why they call it passing out.

Today on the plane? That was violent and harsh and rocked through me like an earthquake.

But that's not something I feel compelled to share.

Since Brayden has said nothing more, I

rush to bolster my lie. "It was just the heat from waiting on the tarmac without the air-conditioning and the fact that I hadn't eaten all day. I swear. And now that you've fed me, the risk of further fainting is practically nil."

In keeping with the wide-eyed new girl in the city cliche, I'd begged Brayden to take me to dinner in Times Square. We ended up at Juniors, where I'd stuffed myself with potato pancakes and followed that up with a huge slice of cheesecake. Only after I was well-fed and had soaked up the carnival atmosphere of Times Square did I tell him about the fainting thing.

Now, I'm regretting that confession, because while I'm happy to move on to drinks at a less touristy location, I do not want that location to be his Upper East Side apartment.

"Manhattan and its many fine drinking establishments will still be here tomorrow," he says.

"I'm fine. Really." I hook my arm

through his. "And you've got to dive back into studying tomorrow, so please, please, pretty please, take me out on the town." I plaster on a winsome smile, then tilt my head up and bat my eyelashes at him.

For a moment I think he's going to turn all serious med student on me. But then he snorts out laughter. "You're insane, you know that right?"

I let go of his arm, even as his expression crumbles. "God, Jay," he says. "I'm so sorry."

"It's okay," I manage a wobbly smile. "It's just an expression."

We both know that's not true, though. Not for me.

As my best friend since second grade, Brayden is one of the few people who knows how bad it was for me as a kid growing up with a certifiably insane mother, and how much worse it got when I was seventeen and she checked out completely by slicing her own throat with a kitchen knife, leaving me numb and my already invisible father a lost shell of himself.

More than that, Brayden is one of the few people who knows that I'm terrified that I'll go down that dark path just like she did.

He twines his fingers with mine and squeezes. "Of course I'll buy you a drink." His voice is gentle, but not overly so, which I appreciate. "Come on. Let's get a taxi back to my place. There's a bar just a few doors down, and I've got a thing for one of the waitresses. You can use your feminine intuition and tell me if she's into me."

"If you can't tell, that means she's not into you."

"Probably," he says. "But I'm practicing optimism."

I cock my head. "How's that going for you?"

"Ask me after we see how I do with the waitress."

I shoulder butt him, my mood improving by the second. "What are you doing dating, anyway? I thought med students spent all their time hunched over cadavers or textbooks. Except, of course, on the day when their best friend arrives in town."

"I never said I wanted to date her." His grin is wicked. "Some people work out by lifting weights. I have other methods."

"Hound dog," I say, but with a laugh.

"True that." He steps into the street and expertly hails a taxi. "And there are aerobic benefits, too. Give it a try. If you can't find a pilates class you like, you can just pick up a guy."

He hops into the taxi that has pulled up beside us before I have time to think of a snappy comeback. I follow, remembering how much I've missed him. Brayden and I have never frolicked between the sheets, and that's fine with me. He's my best friend, and I'm not interested in him joining the ranks of guys I close myself off from.

Because unlike Brayden, who can fuck around and somehow manage to keep all those women on his Christmas card list, I burn bridges. I go out, maybe even go to bed. But I don't get involved.

I told Brayden once that I'd gotten my heart broken too many times, but that is one of the few lies I've ever told him. The truth is, I've never gotten my heart broken because I never let my heart get engaged. My fear isn't that it's going to get broken again, but that it'll get broken in the first place.

I learned a long time ago that I can't get close to people. Even people who love you are primed to hurt you. Maybe because that's just what people do. Or maybe they'll get close enough to see a hint of the crazy inside me. Either way, people aren't the kind of risk I take. If I'm going to have big emotional moments, I'll have them on stage and through someone else's eyes.

Brayden's an exception, and that's only because he snuck into my life when I was too young to know better. Honestly, I'm glad he did. Intellectually, I know I should open up more to the world. Emotionally, I figure so long as I've got Brayden then I can skate a little bit longer before the cracks in my thin emotional ice finally give way.

"You know how much I appreciate this, right?" I say to him now, overcome with warm and fuzzy feelings.

"The drinks? Thank me if you want, but even with you fainting all over the city, I wasn't hard to convince."

"I'm talking about the whole thing. Letting me stay with you until I get a real job, subsidizing the groceries since my contribution would be pretty much limited to ramen. The whole shebang."

"I like ramen. And you do have a real job. Playing Juliet at Story Street is huge."

"Too bad the salary's not." The money really does suck. But being cast in a Story Street production is an amazing opportunity. The theater is equity-waiver and so off, off Broadway that it's in Brooklyn, but it's gained a reputation over the last five years for putting on high quality shows. And a pretty decent percentage of the actors who cross its stage have gone on to the bright lights of actual Broadway productions.

And that, of course, is my dream. Because the only time I truly feel like myself is when I'm on stage playing a character.

It's a short drive, and soon enough Bray leans forward to tell the cabbie where to pull over. As soon as we're out of the taxi, I glance around and am proud of myself for recognizing Brayden's block. We're not going to his building, though, but to a small bar with a sandwich board in front advertising five-dollar well drinks and half-price appetizers until closing.

I grin. I may be mooching off my best friend, but even I can afford to buy us a couple of drinks tonight.

I'm about to tell him as much, when I see a tall woman step out from the shadows just past the bar. She has a dancer's body and long blonde hair. I'm certain I've never seen her before, and yet there is something familiar about her.

I pause, trying to figure it out, and as I do, a car passes. Its headlights must hit her at an odd angle, because in that moment it looks as though her face is made entirely out of flame—and the illusion turns my blood to ice.

"Jay?"

I realize that I've frozen in place. "Sorry. I'm more tired than I thought." I hope that's true. Because right then I feel like I did on the plane, when my entire body had lurched as if I'd been punched in the gut. The ground rose up to meet me, and something seemed to be pulling me out of myself. In that moment, I felt as though I was being yanked through a hole in space, molecule by molecule by molecule. And then, dammit, it had seemed as if my whole body exploded.

It wasn't a nice feeling and not one that I'm keen on repeating, and so I shake myself firmly, then glance back to where I'd seen her only moments before. But no one is there now.

I feel beads of sweat pop along the nape of my neck, and suddenly I want nothing more than to be inside, safe in Brayden's apartment. "Can we skip the drink after all? Maybe have something at your place and put in a movie? I'm just—"

"Tired."

"Yes." I latch gratefully onto the excuse.

"No prob. I've got all sorts of mindless crap we can watch. Or you can just crash. Won't hurt my feelings." He points ahead, more or less in the direction where I'd seen the flaming female. "I'm just three doors down."

"Great." I take his hand, feeling stupid for being scared of what had surely been nothing more than a trick of the light. But then something dark and gray shoots past us and I jump about a mile.

"Just a cat," Bray says. "In fact, I think it's Roger."

"Roger?"

"My neighbor's spoiled ball of fluff. She's a sweet old lady with a ground floor flat in the building next to mine. It has a tiny patio, and she insists on letting Roger go out there even though she freaks out every time he scales the wall. Hang on." He pulls out his phone and uses it as a flashlight, shining it into the small service alley between the bar and the next building over. "Hey, Roger," he says gently. "Come on, buddy."

"It's him?" I'm crouched behind him, my hand resting on his back.

"Yeah. Let me see if I can get him. We'll call it my good deed for the year."

The alley is about as wide as a car, and as I follow him past a collection of rather pungent smelling garbage cans, we pass a heavy door that I assume opens to the bar's kitchen. A single bulb above the door emits a dim light that ostensibly illuminates the alley, but really only makes the shadows deeper.

I hear a rustling behind me and turn, expecting to find Roger. Instead, it's the flame lady.

The first thing I notice is that her face looks normal.

The second thing is the knife in her hand.

I scream and stumble backward even as the big gray blob of a cat launches itself from the top of a trashcan and connects with her face.

The knife goes flying, but that doesn't deter the woman, whose fingers close around my upper arm.

In that freakish trick of time, everything seems to slow and the world is suddenly clearer than it has ever been.

I feel the pressure of her fingers.

I see the cat hissing from behind a plastic crate.

I hear Brayden calling my name.

And I see a strange, colorful blade of light slice sideways from behind the woman, neatly lopping off her head to reveal the tall, dark, god of a warrior wielding a sword behind her.

What the fuck?

Some part of me thinks that I have snapped. That whatever bit of crazy I have inherited from my mother has battled its way to the surface and is all set to drag me back under.

Except I don't believe that. This doesn't

feel like crazy—which is a ridiculous rationalization, when you get right down to it. I mean, if you are losing your mind, chances are you believe that you're perfectly sane.

Even so, I am not worried about my sanity. And, frankly, I don't have time to be concerned about my *laissez-faire* attitude toward these strange goings-on. Time has snapped back into place, and there is a body falling to the ground, and Brayden has my hand and he is yanking me toward the back of the alley where, presumably, there is another way out.

We don't even make it one step.

The warrior holds up a hand, and the air seems suddenly charged. It rolls toward us in waves, its force knocking us both backward. Me against the brick wall and Braydon to the ground. I see him hit his head, and I cry out, afraid he's been knocked unconscious, but the air is so thick that the sound can't even travel.

Then the wave dissipates and I'm left

gasping as the warrior approaches me, that strange, sword-like weapon tight in his hand.

I tilt my head back, breathing hard.

I realize with some surprise that I'm not scared. On the contrary, everything seems oddly familiar. Like *deja vu* on steroids.

And in that moment, I am certain that the fierce looking warrior with the sad gray eyes is going to kill me. More than that, I'm certain that he has killed me before, which really makes no sense whatsoever.

I open my mouth to beg him to stop, but that is not the word that comes out.

Instead, I hear myself saying, "Malcolm?"

CHAPTER 3

*M*ALCOLM.

I don't know how, but I am certain that is the man's name.

More than that, I am certain that he entered this alley tonight intending to kill me.

I know it the same way that I know that the weapon he still has pressed against my neck is called a fire sword.

How I know all that, though, is a mystery, and not one that I need to be solving at the moment.

Right now, I just need to stay alive.

"Mal," I say as my heart pounds wildly. "Please."

I force myself to stand straight. To face him.

He is taller than me, well over six feet with hair as dark as midnight and gray eyes that glint like silver in the dim light.

Right now, there is heat in those eyes. And something else that I think might be regret.

Other than his eyes, this man is stone, his face chiseled perfection, all hard lines and angles softened only slightly by the dark shadow of beard stubble. My first impression had been of a warrior god, and I'd been right. This is a man who knows power. Who knows control.

This is a man who will do what he wants, take what he wants.

And yet for some inexplicable reason, I am not afraid.

As if in acknowledgment of that perplexing realization, he lowers the blade.

This is my chance.

I should scream. I should run.

And yet I do neither of those things. I

just stand there, feeling a bit like I had on the airplane, as if I'm being drawn atom by atom from one reality into another.

"Do you know your name?" There is a tightness in his voice, as if my answer is the most important thing in the world.

"Of course I do." *It's Jaynie*, I think. But that is not what I say. Because that is not my name. Not here. Not with this man. "I'm Christina."

The sword clatters to the ground as a shudder runs through him.

Once again, I think that I should run. Once again, I don't.

Instead I stand there, watching the riot of emotion play across his face. Astonishment. Relief. *Fear?*

And then those emotions are swept away, replaced by a sensual hunger so powerful that it makes my skin tingle in both anticipation and awareness.

"Christina." He says my name sweetly, as if it is a prayer, then clutches my arm and pulls me to him.

I gasp. There's nothing sweet now. This is hard and hot. This is power and demand and the insisting press of his body against mine.

One of his hands finds the small of my back, sliding beneath the thin material of my T-shirt to find the bare skin above the waistband of my skirt.

The touch is electric, and sparks of awareness ricochet through me, like a supernova in my soul. I don't understand what is happening. All I know is that I want this. That I need it.

That I've missed it.

Whatever apprehension I'd felt before is gone, wiped away by the intensity of my reaction to this man. And oh, dear god, is it intense. My skin prickles with need, sensitive even to the gentle brush of air. My breasts are heavy, my nipples hard. My sex is swollen, throbbing in anticipation of his touch.

But it is my lips that crave him the most. And in a motion that makes me believe that he has the power to read my mind, he swoops down and claims my mouth in a kiss that is wild and hard desperate. I yield willingly, my lips parting in welcome. In his arms, my body goes limp as I surrender, trusting him to keep me upright as our teeth clash and our tongues mate in a primal frenzy that has my pulse pounding so hard in my ears I can hear nothing else.

This can't be reality because there is no way that I can feel this light, this free, this *found*. And yet I do, and it's real, and I know by the taste of his kisses and the brush of his hand upon my skin that it's right. It's familiar.

It's home.

I don't understand it. All I know is that I have missed him. I need him. And I have to have him—hard and fast and now.

Almost violently, he breaks the kiss, pulling back and breathing hard, and I fear that whatever madness has claimed us both is over.

"Please." The word escapes me before I

have time to think. "Please, don't stop."

His mouth curves up into a smile so sensual it is almost a caress. "Stop? Lover, we haven't even begun."

The endearment sends shivers through me, and I draw in a breath, overwhelmed by the sensation that there is a whole world just beyond my peripheral vision, and if only I could turn my head, then I could see it. Return to it.

I can't think about that, though. Not now while his fingertips are brushing lightly over my forehead, my lips, my cheeks, as if he is memorizing every curve and angle of my face. It's a gentle touch, but it is driving me wild, and it takes all my willpower to stay still when all I want is the sensation of his body pressed hard against mine. Touching me. Taking me. Filling me.

"Dear god, how I've missed you."

I hear the sadness in his voice and want to weep. "Me, too," I whisper, meaning the words even though I do not understand them.

"You remember, then?"

"I—" A tremor of fear runs through me, and in that moment I don't want to remember. Even if remembering means that I would understand. Even if it means that Mal will fill my thoughts and my dreams and my memories.

But there are wisps. Tiny threads of memory that seem to float by, almost close enough to grasp. And they are filled with fire and heat. With caresses and passion.

With Mal.

I meet his eyes. "All I remember is you." Warm tears snake down my cheeks as the memories form a tapestry of images and sensations. His lips. His hands. Our flesh, our souls, our very beings entwined in passion. "I don't—" My breath hitches. I don't understand what's going on, not any of it. In that moment, I know only the man. His heat. His touch. His fire.

I'm lost in a dark mist, but Mal is at the end of a brightly lit path, and if I can just run to him, then I'll be out of the mist. I'll be safe.

And I'm trying. I'm trying so hard. But the mist is gathering closer, filling in the spaces between us and threatening to take him away from me.

The thought is unbearable, and I reach for him, fisting my hands in his shirt, then levering myself toward him. "Touch me," I demand. "Touch me, please, before you lose me again."

It is as if I have opened a door. Had I thought his kisses were wild before? They were tame compared to this.

This kiss is frenzied. Savage.

It is a promise. A confession.

It's a reunion—I know it. I feel it. And though I don't understand it, I go with it. Because right now, this man is all I want. And I am afraid, so desperately afraid, that he is about to be ripped away from me.

He slams me back against the wall, and I cry out, both in need and in surprise. His hand snakes under my skirt, stroking my skin as he pushes it higher and higher. My breath hitches in my throat, and I bite down on my lower lip to keep myself from begging him for more. For everything.

"My love." The tender words are a growl of passion. "I don't want it to be like this, outside in an alley. But I can't wait. After so long, dammit, Christina, I have to have you."

"Yes. Oh, god, Mal. Please. Now, please." I am wild. I am frantic. I am lust and need.

I am his.

"Please," I beg again. "I need more. Mal, I need *you*."

He roughly shoves my panties aside, then thrusts his fingers inside me. I am wet—so very wet—and he enters me easily.

I tilt my head back and gasp in ecstasy as my vagina clenches tight around his fingers, wanting him deeper. Hell, just wanting more.

I bring my hands up between us, and force his shirt open, not caring that I'm ripping to shreds a garment that probably cost more than I will ever make in a month. I have to touch him. Right now, I am certain that if I cannot touch flesh against flesh, I will shrivel up and die. And as soon as I have exposed his chest, bare except for the vibrant tattoo of a phoenix rising from flames, I press my palm flat against him, and close my eyes as his heart beat thrums through me, keeping time with my own.

He closes his hands over mine, and I moan a bit in protest, because his fingers are no longer inside me. But when he takes my hands and draws them up over my head, I cease protesting. "Stay like that," he says, even as he turns his attention to my shirt. He tugs up the hem, then makes short work of the clasp at the front of my bra. Then he cups his hands around my rib cage and closes his mouth over my left breast.

I sigh with pleasure, craving more, knowing without understanding how long it has been since I have had his touch. Since I have felt this connection.

"My love…"

His words are as soft as the lips that trail down my body, making my muscles twitch and shudder in both anticipation and pleasure. Slowly, he eases lower and lower until he reaches the waistband of my skirt. It is a full cotton skirt, with an elastic waist and deep pockets into which I've shoved my phone and credit card. It had fallen back down when he'd drawn his hands up me, and now he hikes it up again, using his hands to lift it so that there is a pool of material gathered at my waist.

"I've missed this. Your taste. The sensation of your skin against my lips, my fingers. I don't ever want to stop touching you. I want to make up for all the lost years—god, so many lost years." His voice is hard. Urgent. "We didn't have long enough before they took you—not nearly long enough."

"No," I whisper, knowing that he is right, though I do not understand why.

He hesitates only long enough to tilt his head back up to look at me, and I draw in a sharp breath, awed by the heat of the vibrant passion I see in his slate gray eyes. And then he lowers his head and kisses me right above the band of the tiny panties I am wearing.

I tremble with pleasure, reflexively arching up even as I widen my stance.

"Hold your skirt," he demands, and I do without hesitation, then almost weep from the overwhelming eroticism of the cool night air brushing my sensitive sex as he eases my underwear to one side. And when he kisses me so intimately, his tongue teasing my clit even as his hands stroke my inner thighs and climb higher and higher, I am absolutely certain that I am going to melt with a pleasure more intense than anything I have experienced before.

Except it's not enough. Dear god, it's not nearly enough.

"Please." I drop the skirt, twining my hands in his hair and easing him up. "I need more. Oh, god Mal, I need you."

Yes.

I do not hear the word. I only see the movement of his mouth. How can I hear when my heart is pounding so wildly?

He picks me up as if I am weightless and clutches me to him as my legs tighten around his hips. He turns around so that his back is to the wall and holds me so that I am sitting on one hand and his other is cupping my back.

I do not know when he managed it, but his jeans are undone, and his erection is hot and hard between my legs. I close my eyes and bite my lower lip. I want this, dammit. I want it *now*.

"Your panties," he says. "Pull them aside."

I start to do that, but he is impatient, and he removes his hand from my back long enough to reach around and tear them free. I cry out, almost coming right then simply from the wild violence of the moment. But that is nothing compared to the way I feel when he tells me to hold on to his shoulders and lock my legs. When he guides his cock to my core. When he takes hold of my hips and thrusts down, impaling me on him even as he tilts his pelvis up, so that he is deeper in me than I could possibly have imagined.

I arch back, my fingers laced behind his neck, and my legs locked around his hips. I want to feel him deeper. I want to feel him completely. I want to be filled by this man, body, heart and mind, and as we piston together—as I move in sync and our sounds of pleasure rise like a symphony—I know that finally, *finally*, we are one, he and I.

Just as we are supposed to be.

Even as the thought crashes through me, the world seems to explode, vibrant and alive with light and color.

I am soaring. I am free. I am alive.

And I remember.

Not in bits and pieces or incongruent flashes. But full-on. A flood. Hell, a tsunami of thoughts and memories and emotions.

Mal and Liam and Jessica and Raine and so many others. My mate. My friends.

The shock of disassembling. Of leaving our own world, our own dimension. Of traveling so far, so fast.

The fear that we would be too late—that the fuerie would escape, and we would not only fail in our mission, but would bear witness to the destruction of the very core of existence.

And I remember the pain and horror when everything shifted. When the rift opened and we were thrust across the void into the wrong place, the wrong time, the wrong world.

I remember the sensual electric sensation when we merged with the humans and were made flesh, and then the sweet surrender when I fell into Mal's open arms. Of Mal's eyes looking deep into mine. Of thinking *yes, yes, of course he would take that form, lean and powerful and strong.* And I remember the way my new body responded to his, melting against him and merging with him in a wild and wonderful dance of passion and claiming. And—most of all—of love.

I remember the battle, cold and hard and tenacious.

I remember loss and capture, torture and

pain.

And I remember Mal's face, wretched with agony. The strain in his voice as he held me, battered and broken. As he told me that he would fix it—that he wouldn't let them use me. That I would never become the instrument of death that the fuerie intended. That he would do what must be done, and that I needed to know that he loved me always.

That he would protect me.

That he would keep the world safe, both from me and for me.

That somehow he would find a way to save me.

And then I remember the tears that welled in his eyes as he held me in his arms, engaged his fire sword, and with a cry of pain that even now sends a shiver through me, thrust his weapon through my heart.

CHAPTER 4

A SCREAM RIPS the air, and it takes a moment for me to realize that not only is it mine, but that it is being forced from me not just by the pressure of my lungs, but also by a boiling, writhing energy that seems to be welling up inside of me. Not fear, but fomented by it. Not pain, but unlocked by it.

And even as I realize that, a new terror washes over me. And not simply the loss and horror of the realization that Mal betrayed me—this man whose touch fills me with such delight and whose memory I hold so dear. But another terror. Colder. Darker. And bitter with blood.

This is it. This is the evil they put inside me.

And relief sweeps over me as I realize that this is why Mal destroyed me. Not to betray, but to protect. To save not only me, but the world.

And I am about to destroy all of that because I do not have the strength to control what is now boiling within me.

Back it off.

Breathe—just breathe. And back it the fuck off.

Even as I think that, I know that it is impossible. I can't stop this power—this pounding, pulsing, violent energy. I can't control it, and soon it will explode out of me, destroying not only me and Mal and Brayden, but everyone near this alley, this street, this whole fucking continent.

It's rising—rising—

And I'm scared. So damn terrified. And I curl my hands into fists, grabbing tight to Mal's shirt, but it doesn't help, because how could that help when all this power just wants to shoot out of me, and I can feel the heat building in me, like a volcano about to erupt? Hotter and hotter, and wilder and deeper until it's going to just—just—

Stop.

It's gone.

Just *whoosh*, like someone let the air out of a balloon, and I realize that I am a shell. That every ounce of energy has been drained from me. Even the part of me that was feeding the volcano.

I don't know how. I don't know why. I only know that I lack the strength to stand. My knees buckle and I sag toward the ground, only to be captured before I fall in the arms of——oh, holy Christ, I can't remember his name. But he is staring at me with an expression that seems to be fear mixed with concern mixed with tenderness.

"I—Do I know you?"

For a moment, he doesn't move. Not a muscle. Not a breath.

And then, very slowly, he shakes his head. "No," he says. "You don't know me."

I swallow. I'm not scared, though some part of me thinks that I should be. On the contrary, with his hand at my back I feel safer than I have ever felt in my life.

But that evaporates in a heartbeat when I realize that not only are my clothes askew, but that Brayden is splayed out motionless on the asphalt. I jerk in shock, and when I do I catch a glimpse of what is behind the man who holds me. A body—and oh dear god help me—it's headless.

Panic shoots through me. Ice and frost fill every part of me until I am frozen with fear, literally unable to move.

"Please." I force the word out. "Please don't hurt me."

He flinches, as if my words are a slap. Then he very gently sets me on the ground.

I scramble to Brayden's side, then exhale with relief when I see his chest rising and falling.

When he speaks, the man's voice is soft. Almost a whisper. "No," he says. "I'm not going to hurt you. Not this time."

But I don't believe him, because he is moving toward me with such an expression of desolation it rips my heart out.

Then he presses his fingertips to my forehead, and I slump to the ground, one word ringing in my ears. *Forget*.

MAL'S ENTIRE BODY ached, as if he'd fought a long, hard battle that had ended with someone taking a fist and pounding it into his gut.

Then again, isn't that exactly what had happened? *He'd had her back.* For a few perfect, amazing moments, he'd had Christina back in his arms, perfect and beautiful. Long brown hair that fell in waves just past her shoulders. Deep brown eyes as innocent as a deer's. And oh, god, she had the face of an angel.

She was always pretty—how could a woman with her core be anything but?—but this time she was so lovely it almost hurt.

He'd craved her, mind and body.

Craved her, and for a few grand moments, he'd had her. He'd even gone so far as to allow himself to believe that everything was okay. That after all this time, she'd learned to control it. To battle it down.

To keep the power that was trapped within her safe and dormant and locked away tight.

How fucking wrong he'd been. And dammit, dammit, god-*fucking*-dammit, he knew damn well that he was the reason she'd lost her grip. That he was the one who had ripped the power loose. Who had sent it spiraling up almost to the point of explosion. And it had taken all of his control and strength to keep the whole fucking world from ending.

He'd almost failed.

God help him, he'd been so lost in the feel of her that he had almost been too late.

He'd won, though. In the end, he'd won, at least if you could call it a win. Mal really wasn't sure anymore.

Maybe he'd saved the world by absorbing her energy, but she was lost to him once more.

No longer his mate, but his prey.

Not his lover, but the woman that he had been tasked to kill.

Goddammit all to hell.

A wave of nausea swept over him as he crouched to retrieve his fire sword. Without shifting his gaze from where Christina lay asleep on the ground, he extended the blade, oddly comforted by the familiar vibration of the weapon in his palm.

He lifted it, knowing what he had to do. Knowing that if he didn't take action—if he didn't destroy her yet again—that he was putting not only his race at risk, but this entire world.

One breath, then another.

It was easy. Hadn't he done it a hundred times? A thousand? Just a contraction of his muscles. Just a few moments of heartbreak and then it would be over. He would be free for another decade, another century.

Free, and alone.

Free, and miserable.

He didn't lunge. Didn't bring the sword down and steal this life, this existence, from the woman he loved.

Instead, he deactivated the weapon, then slid it back into the pocket of his jeans.

He stood a moment longer, looking down at the woman and at the man who still slept beside her.

And then Mal, who had never once defied orders or ignored his mission, turned the opposite direction, and walked away.

CHAPTER 5

I WAKE TO the sun streaming through the window, then stretch lazily in the huge bed that dominates the guest suite in Brayden's massive apartment.

I'm naked, and the sensation of the cool sheets sliding over my heated skin is incredible, allowing me to fully enjoy the lingering remnants of a truly exceptional dream.

Sadly, in the way of dreams, I cannot grasp even the tiniest tendril of memory. I know only that the dream was deliciously sensual and starred a gray-eyed man whose face I cannot see no matter how hard I try. Nor can I conjure the sound of his voice.

Just one word lingers—*Lover.*

The thought of it makes me shiver.

I am not prone to erotic dreams, and this morning I can't help but think how unfortunate that is, because I have awakened wet and aroused, and I have to say that I like it.

Bray and I had returned to the apartment after our effort to snare Roger the cat had failed, despite having braved the dark shadows and hideous odors of one of New York City's alleyways.

A full day of travel—punctuated by fainting spells and cheesecake—must have finally taken its toll, and I'm glad that we didn't go for drinks. Considering my exhausted state last night, I can only imagine the kind of hangover I'd now be suffering.

Brayden's parents divorced when he was six, after which Brayden and his newly single mom moved to my neighborhood. But Brayden is a Kline on his father's side—as in the massive hotel chain that has pretty much taken over the Northern hemisphere—and that means that hospitality is in his blood. And *that* means that my room overflows with amenities. Right now, I'm especially appreciative of the fluffy white robe. I put it on, cinch the tie, and stumble from the guest suite into the state of the art kitchen.

I expect to find Brayden there, but of course I've forgotten that he has class. He's left me a note, though, telling me that he's going to stay at school all day to study, but to make myself at home and he'll be there when I get back from rehearsal.

I glance at my watch. It's not yet eleven, and rehearsal doesn't start until three. Even when I factor in changing my clothes, grabbing a bite, and getting to Brooklyn, I have tons of time. What I should do is start scouring the Internet for a day job—I'm thinking about fully embracing the starving actor cliche and waiting tables. Instead, I decide to go for a run.

I'm not one of those people who loves to run and craves the runner's high, which I am convinced is only a myth. I do it for practical and vanity based reasons. Vanity, because it's the best and fastest way to keep my butt and legs looking decent. And practical, because acting is hard work, and the cardio keeps me sharp.

This morning, I'm not thinking about either of those things, though. Instead, I just want to work off this weird energy. This antsy, almost sexual thrum that has been burning through me since I woke up.

That must have been one hell of a dream.

I think about the gray eyes again and wonder to whom they belong. Is he just a figment of my imagination, or am I having sex dreams about someone I met in passing and my subconscious latched onto?

When she was lucid, my mother would have said he was a lover from a past life. For that matter, she'd probably say the same when she wasn't sane.

Either way, he is not real and he is not here, and I tell myself that is a good thing.

But as I make my way to the lobby and then start out down 59th Street at a slow jog,

I can't help but wonder if the man from my dream really does exist. And, if so, what I will do when I meet him.

"TELL ME, DAUGHTER Juliet, how stands your disposition to be married?"

I look across the stage to Angie, the woman who plays Lady Capulet, my mother. "It is an honor I dream not of." I am holding the script in my hand, but I don't have to look at the pages. This is a play that I have loved my entire life. There is something about the romance of it. The tragedy. The star-crossed lovers.

The story called to me the first time I read it in high school, and playing the role of Juliet now is like living in a dream.

Beside me, Juliet's nurse, played by a boisterous woman named Marva, begins her lines. "An honor!" She makes a snorting sound and dives into one of the best deliveries of the rest of her line that I have ever heard. But I am only halfway paying attention. Instead, I am looking off stage, over the rows of seats, to a shadow in the distance.

There's someone there. I'm certain of it.

Someone standing in the shadows and watching me.

"Christina?"

I jerk my head up to face Eric, the director. "Sorry. What?"

"Are we keeping you from a pressing engagement?"

I stand up straighter and give him my full attention, the very epitome of contrition. Because the last thing I want to do is piss off or insult the very first New York director I've worked with. "No. No, of course not. I just—"

"What?"

"I was thinking about Juliet's character," I lie. "She's so young, and of course we know she's a virgin. But she's still quite sophisticated sexually—I mean, if you don't pick up on that before, it's apparent during the balcony scene, right?"

"Wilt thou leave me so unsatisfied," Eric recites, quoting Romeo's line.

"Exactly." I'm practically giddy that he bought my story. "And she flirts back, asking him what satisfaction he can have right then—I mean, she might as well say you can't sleep with me now. I'm holding all the cards." What I don't mention is that this line really has been taunting me. Because after waking up so aroused, I've felt rather unsatisfied myself all day.

"Very true." He nods, and I feel a surge of gratitude for my eleventh grade Honors English teacher who worked with me on my semester paper on the role of women in Shakespeare's plays. Eric shifts his attention to Angie and Marva. "Anything to add, ladies? Other than that our newest member of the company has already proven herself worthy of being a Story Street alumnus?"

As both women sing my praises and comment on their own characters, I glance once again toward the back of the theater. I don't actually expect to see anyone. For one thing, it's highly likely there was no one there at all, and I was just conjuring up remnants from my dream. But even if he was real, he surely would have overheard the conversation and gotten the hell out of here.

So I am not at all prepared when I see the movement in the back row. And not just movement, but a person. A man.

He rises, and because the stage lights are on, I see him only in silhouette. Tall and lean, he stands with the with the kind of confident posture that suggests that he is exactly where he is supposed to be, the rest of the world be damned.

He is looking toward the stage, and though he could be looking at any one of the four of us, I know without a shadow of a doubt that his attention is entirely focused on me.

For a moment, he remains still. But when he finally moves to leave, the houselights catch his eyes. And though I know that he is much too far away for me to really have seen the color, it doesn't matter. Because I am absolutely one-hundred percent sure that they are as gray as a building storm.

Malcolm.

The name cuts through me, and I stop, only then realizing that I'd taken a step toward him.

I shake my head, entirely unsure where that name came from. I don't know anyone named Malcolm, and yet the name seems to fit this man perfectly.

Which, of course, also makes no sense.

I watch as the man turns and leaves, pushing through the double doors at the back of the theater. I'm just about to rattle off an excuse about needing to go to the bathroom when Eric turns a bit and deliberately includes me in the conversation.

"Of course, analysis and interpretation is essential," he says, "but the key is applying that interpretation. So how does what you noted about Juliet's sexual sophistication apply to the scene we're running?"

"Um." I mentally kick myself, because my mind has wandered so far off topic that I'm having a hard time remembering what exactly I noted. "Right," I stall. "Well, they're talking about marriage. And, um, if she's sophisticated about what goes on during a wedding night, then her line should maybe not be delivered with innocence, but with more self-assurance?"

For a moment, he says nothing. Then he points to Alicia. "Let's run through it again. Christina, excellent work."

My cheeks heat, but I accept the compliment graciously. And throughout the rest of rehearsal—as I infuse Juliet's dialogue with sensuality and sexual awareness—I force myself not to think about the gray-eyed man who had filled my dreams.

Or the mysterious man who watched me from the back of the theater.

CHAPTER 6

MAL CONTINUED TO study the chessboard as Liam dropped into the seat across the table from him. They were in the VIP room at Dark Pleasures, the members only club that the Phoenix Brotherhood had established in 1895 after Mal had insisted that they needed a place to gather, to talk, to be among friends.

Not that the club at 36 East 63rd Street was limited only to the brotherhood. On the contrary, throughout the years they had offered private memberships to certain select humans, most of whom didn't have the slightest inkling that their hosts had more secrets than simply what transpired behind the solid oak door that led to the VIP section. The policy was useful in a number of ways, most specifically because it allowed the brotherhood to keep its finger on the pulse of the city, not to mention the world. Dark Pleasures's clientele was, after all, highly exclusive. And any given evening would find the bar filled with politicians and dealmakers, money men and celebrities.

Today was Saturday, and since it was still early, Liam and Mal were the only two people in the VIP room. Later the brotherhood would fill this room, and members would flood the main clubroom. The air would be pungent with the scent of fine cigars, and the sound of ice tingling in highball glasses would fill the air. Most weekends he made the rounds through the members' area, often finding a woman to share his bed that night.

Tonight, that wasn't going to happen.

After having Christina in his arms only two nights ago, he knew he would never again be inclined to bed another woman, not even for the pleasure of forgetting.

"Who's winning?" Liam asked, nodding at the chessboard.

Mal sighed as he picked up his queen and rolled her between his fingers. "I suppose that depends on what qualifies as a win."

"Considering you're playing yourself, that's not the answer I expected."

Mal put the queen back down, taking care not to look at his friend's face. "I've been playing by myself for a long damn time, Liam."

"Yeah," Liam said softy. "I guess you have."

Mal looked up, then took a long sip of Glenlivet as he studied his friend. Liam's broad shoulders and well-muscled body filled the chair, but equally compelling was his commanding presence. Liam was a man who knew what he wanted, and didn't stop until he got it.

Mal and Liam were like brothers and had been for millennia. Hell, since before they'd left home to come here, chasing the bad guys across time and space like goddamn cowboys. And now here they both were, co-leaders of the Phoenix Brotherhood, a group of immortal warriors headquartered in New York, but scattered across the globe. Still chasing the bad guys. Still trying to put right what had gotten fucked up so many centuries ago.

He almost laughed. Put like that, it sounded like the plot of a goddamn James Cameron movie.

Liam pulled out his phone and placed it on the table. "Just heard from Raine."

Interested, Mal leaned back in the leather armchair. Mal and Raine had been friends since their training days, but that friendship rose to a new level when they'd both lost their mates as a result of the shit storm that had gone down when they'd crashed in this dimension. Livia, thrust back into the rift between dimensions. Christina, an unwilling host for a horrific and unstable weapon.

Both men had been desperately lonely,

their pain acting almost like a bond. But recently Raine had learned that Livia's essence hadn't been catapulted out of this world after all. Instead, it had been absorbed into a human, and after all these years, Raine had once again found his mate's essence in the body and soul of Callie Sinclair.

And though Mal was happy for his friend—truly happy—he couldn't deny that he was jealous as fuck. Because he was never getting Christina back. Not like that. Maybe he'd given her a reprieve—letting her live her life and go to her rehearsals and take her jogs in Central Park and go out for sushi with the friend she'd moved in with, because oh yes, he'd been watching her—but that was just time, and time was running out. She was a walking bomb about to go supernova, and she didn't even know it. And sooner—not later—he was going to have to man up and pull the damn trigger.

Unless…

"Mal?" Liam's voice was steady, but Mal could hear the concern. And the question.

"Thinking. Sorry." He rubbed his chin, the stubble scratching his palm and reminding him that he hadn't shaved in days. Not since seeing Christina had thrown his life completely off-kilter. He sucked in air and ordered himself to get his shit together. "Is Raine on his way here?"

Liam nodded. "They're coming in before they go celebrate. Callie's now a New York County Assistant District Attorney."

"That's excellent." Before coming to New York to be with her ailing father, Callie had been a lawyer in Texas. Once she and Raine found each other, though, she'd taken steps to secure a similar position in Manhattan so that she could continue the job she enjoyed while being with the man she loved.

Mal glanced down at the table to hide the spike of jealousy and considered the position of the rook in relation to the bishop. "It can only help Phoenix Security to have someone in the DA's office."

"Agreed," Liam said, and then said nothing else.

Mal closed his eyes, silently cursing. He loved Liam like a goddamn brother, but right then he just wanted to be alone. He opened his eyes and put his elbow on the table, then rested his chin on his fist. He studied the board and hoped that Liam would get the hint.

Liam didn't move.

When the weight of the silence became too much, Mal looked up at him. "Something else?"

"I don't know. Is there?"

Mal said nothing, just waited.

"Dammit, Mal, you need to talk to me. You've been brooding for two days. Either wandering the streets off god knows where or sitting over this damn chessboard, half the time without an opponent."

"There's always an opponent," Mal said.

"Jessica's worried," Liam said, referring to his own mate.

At that, Mal bit back a smile. "Jessica?"

"Fine. I'm worried, too. Tell me I don't

have reason to be."

Mal sighed, then combed his fingers through his hair. "I've been thinking about games," he admitted, knowing that Liam would understand that he was thinking about Christina. Because when was Mal *not* thinking about Christina? "About strategies."

"Mal. Don't do this to yourself."

"To myself?" A sudden fury burst through him, and he lashed out, sending chess pieces flying. "Do you think I want this pain? Dammit, Liam, not a day goes by that I don't think of her. That I don't crave the moment when I will see her again ... even as I dread it."

Liam drew in a breath. "I wish I didn't have to tell you this. But she's back. She's in New York."

Mal's body turned to ice. Each time Christina was born into this world—humans would call it reincarnation—her physical form was different. As her mate, only Mal could sense her essence from afar. But the members of the brotherhood—all of them, including Jessica and the other immortal women—could sometimes catch a glimpse of the weapon hidden deep inside her if they were looking straight at her. Some, like Asher, could even feel the disturbance in the fabric of the universe when the power of the weapon rose up inside her.

Mal clenched and unclenched his fists as he gathered himself. Thank god Asher had been out of the country last Thursday night. He'd been too far away to feel the ripples in the universe.

But the question remained—what did Liam know? And how?

"Did you hear me?" Liam asked. "She's back."

"Are you sure?"

In front of him, Liam's face was harsh. "Dante saw her. He said it was just a flicker, so he could be wrong, but—"

"He's not," Mal said flatly, as the cold settled into his bones. He turned his attention to the now empty chessboard.

"Do you think it doesn't destroy me, too? She was your mate, but she was my friend, my crew. But there's no other way," Liam said, accurately following Mal's thoughts. "There is no other strategy, no trick we haven't thought of."

He stood, and Mal could see the pain on his friend's face, as potent as his own. "You have to kill her again, Mal. Because if you don't, she'll end up destroying us all."

"Do you think I don't know that? Jesus, Liam, I think about it every goddamn day."

Liam tilted his head, his eyes narrowing as he studied his friend. Mal silently cursed. Liam was not an idiot. And one of the reasons he was a damn good leader was because he saw what his crew—and what his partner—tried to hide.

"You've seen her," Liam said, as he rose out of the chair, as if the news had pushed him to his feet. "You've seen her, and you let it ride. Goddammit, Mal." He pressed the fingertips of both hands to his temples. "If you don't do it, I will. The stakes are too damn high."

Without even thinking about it, Mal was out of his chair, his fist slamming hard into his friend's jaw. As a man, Liam was huge, wide and muscular compared to Mal's lean, athletic frame. And Liam had at least forty pounds on him.

Didn't matter. Mal caught him unaware and sent him stumbling backward, then fisted his hand in the collar of Liam's shirt and yanked him back. "Do not even *think* of going there."

Liam said nothing, but Mal could feel the tension in his friend as Liam held back, forcing himself to stay still. Mal wished he wouldn't. He wanted Liam to let go. Goddammit, right then he wanted nothing more than to beat the shit out of somebody. Anybody.

"Mal!"

He looked up to see Callie across the room, her green eyes seeming even wider with her blond hair pulled back into an elegant knot, and Raine moving fast toward them.

"Back it off, buddy," Raine said. His tight expression, sleeves of tats, and close-shaved head would have made him seem dangerous if Mal didn't know him so well. Then again, Raine *was* dangerous. Just not to the brotherhood.

"*No*," Liam said, his eyes never leaving Mal's face. "You need to do it, then do it. Take a swing at me. Beat me to a bloody pulp. Do whatever you have to, but get it out of your goddamn system. Because you know I'm right, Mal."

Time seemed to stop as Mal stood there, his hand still locked on Liam's shirt. Beside him, Raine stood poised to intervene, clearly torn, not sure if he should be pulling Mal back or following Liam's lead and just letting this little drama play out.

And across the room, Callie watched all three of them, her lovely face awash in horror and confusion.

"Goddammit." Anguish flooded him, and Mal dropped his hand, releasing Liam.

Once more, he sank back into the chair, then covered his face with his hands and told himself that the only thing he needed to do in that moment was remember to breathe.

"She's back," Raine said. It wasn't a question, and Mal didn't answer.

"Who?" Callie's voice was soft and near.

"Christina."

"Oh, Mal." Sorrow filled her voice. "I'm so sorry."

He looked up. Raine had taken the chair beside Mal, and he held out his hand for Callie, who settled in his lap.

"You told her?" he asked Raine, then sighed as his friend nodded. "Do you remember Christina?" he asked the Callie.

Callie shook her head. "It's not like that. I know there's part of Livia inside me, but it's not memories so much as feelings." She looked between the men. "Isn't it that way for her, too?"

"Christina never remembers a thing," Liam said.

"No." Mal met Liam's eyes. "This time, she remembered."

"What?" He could hear the shock in Liam's voice.

"Jesus, Mal," Raine said.

"Wait." Callie looked between the three men. "I'm a little behind the curve here. She remembers you? How do you know?"

Mal hesitated, but he knew he had to come clean. He looked from Raine to Liam. "I went to her. When I felt her presence, I went to her, just like I always have. And dammit, I had every intention of—" He closed his eyes. "She said my name." He drew in a breath. "I touched her, Li. I held her. I—"

He cut himself off, remembering. God, he'd taken her in a fucking alley. After so long, and that was how he'd touched her, how he'd claimed her? She deserved so much more, but he hadn't been able to hold back.

For that matter, she hadn't been able to either, and the memory brought a hint of a smile to his lips. At least she'd been as crazed as he had. And seeing that—finally having proof that she was still herself even inside this new body, that she was still his— had both ripped him to shreds and given him hope.

Right now, it was that hope to which he clung so desperately.

He looked at his friends. "She was mine." He spoke firmly, knowing that they all understood exactly what he meant by that. "And everything came back to her. She remembered me. Remembered us. She knew what was happening and why. And then—"

From the corner of his eye, he saw Callie take Raine's hand and squeeze as tears glistened in her eyes.

"What?" Liam demanded. His voice was businesslike. Practical. But Mal could see the way Liam's fingers were digging into the arm of the chair.

"She almost lost it."

"Oh, Christ," Liam said. "Oh, *fuck*."

"No." Mal stood, because he needed to

get this out. He'd been thinking—god, how much he'd been thinking over the past two days. "No, I pulled it back. I absorbed it—not the weapon. But her own energy. I backed it down, and the darkness fell away, too."

"You backed it down?"

Mal nodded at Callie. "It's what I'm especially good at. Absorbing energy, then turning it around for my own purpose."

"The way Raine is with electronics."

Mal nodded. "Takes me hours to talk to a computer, but he can do it in a nano-second."

"So when you took her energy, it left her exhausted, so the weapon thing couldn't, um, detonate?"

"Something like that." He didn't mention that the effort it had taken was brutal, and that he almost hadn't managed in time. What he did say was, "That's when she forgot. Who I was. What had happened to her. To us." He dragged his fingers through his hair. "That was my opportunity. I had the chance to do it right then. To buy us another few decades, maybe a century. But I didn't take it. I took her memory of what happened in that alley, and I left her there."

"You left her," Liam repeated.

"Don't worry. I kept surveillance on her. No one's getting to her without going through us." Mal knew well that the fuerie wanted the weapon back. And that meant that it wanted Christina. And once it knew that she was alive again in the world, it would do anything to reacquire her. To keep her. And, when the time was right, to use the weapon inside her.

Of course, one of the brotherhood, Dante, had the ability to reach out and search for the unique disturbance in the air caused by the fuerie's energy spectrum. He couldn't pinpoint them around the globe, but if any of the fuerie were near, he could pick up on their vibration. That skill, however, required Dante to purposefully reach out and was limited geographically. In other words, a handy trick, but with limited usefulness.

To be safe, Mal needed eyes on Christina at all times. And thank goodness she was living in a building with excellent security.

"Fuck, man," Liam said. "Do you know the goddamn risk—of course you know the risk. What the hell were you thinking?"

Mal ignored the question. "I've taken most shifts, and when it's not me, I've kept one of the red teams on her," he said, referring to the elite ex-military operatives that Phoenix Security, the brotherhood's front company, kept on the payroll. "But yes, I walked away, and I left her alive. And I've come here, and I've thought, and I've planned."

He bent to retrieve a fallen chess piece, then sat in the armchair again, the white queen in his hand. "I can't do it anymore, Liam. And I won't let anyone else do it, either."

"Won't let?" Liam's brow rose.

"There are other options." He put the queen on the table. "There are other ways to win this game."

"Dammit, Mal. We just had this conversation. You know—"

"Hold up, Li," Raine said. "Could you destroy Jessica? Take a blade to her over and over and over again? Can you even imagine what it's like to lose her? I can," he said, tightening his arms around Callie. "And Mal's had it a thousand times worse. So if he says there's another way, then we need to at least hear him out."

He turned to Mal. "We all know she's dangerous, so I'm not saying that we're going to jump all over whatever you suggest. But I am saying we should let you make your case."

As Raine spoke, some of the tightness in Mal's chest loosened. The brotherhood wasn't a democracy—what Liam and Mal agreed was law, and where they disagreed, Asher cast the deciding vote. Ash, however, was in transit back from London and not any help at the moment.

But Liam respected Raine. And if nothing else, Mal appreciated his friend having his back.

A moment passed, then another. Then Liam nodded. "All right," he said, turning from Raine to Mal. "What's your plan?"

"Wait," Callie said. "I'm sorry, but I have a few thousand years of catching up to do. What happened to her. Why is she dangerous? And why does killing her buy you decades or centuries?"

Mal met Raine's eyes. "I thought you told her."

"Only that you lost Christina. Only what you've had to do every time she comes back."

"And I know what Raine told me about the brotherhood. About how you were all part of an elite team that left your world—your dimension—on a mission to stop the fuerie."

Raine nodded. "You know how I explained that in our dimension, energy is sentient? You don't need a body?"

"I remember," Callie said. "I still don't

fully understand how that works, but I remember. And you said that the fuerie was like a malevolent energy."

"That's putting it mildly," Liam said.

"But you were chasing it," Callie continued. "And you didn't mean to come here—to this dimension or this planet—but there was a crash, and your group and the fuerie ended up here."

"Those are the high points, yes," Mal said.

Callie nodded slowly, as if gathering her thoughts. "And there was an Egyptian prince who had visions. He knew you were coming, and he sent a delegation to meet your group. He probably believed you were gods, who knows. But for whatever reason, they all willingly merged with you."

"With the members of the brotherhood, yes. Not with the fuerie. We merged at a genetic level. It's what made us human. And our original state—pure energy—is what gives us immortality even as flesh."

"But that didn't happen to Livia or

Christina? There was a battle, and they never ended up doing the merging thing?"

"Livia, yes," Mal said. "And, sadly, a few others of our number. But not Christina. She did merge with a human female. I could touch her. Hold her." Pain raked over him with the memory. "And then they took her."

"Why?"

Mal tried to answer, but could only shake his head.

"They would have taken anyone," Liam said gently. "Christina and Jessica had gone out to tend to some wounded humans. They were ambushed. Jessica managed to escape, but they took Christina."

"We raided their camp that night," Raine said. "But they had already used her."

"Used her?"

"Not sexually. As a repository for the weapon. It was the weapon we were hunting even more than the fuerie itself."

"What is it?" she asked.

"Nothing that's yet been discovered in this world. Dark matter. Scalar energy. The scientists studying those are on the right path."

"And they made it part of her?"

"Bound it with her essence," Mal said, drawing a deep breath. "Her energy. Her soul." He stood, not able to sit while he told this part. "We got her back after the raid, but it was too late. Energy has to be contained in this world—the fuerie had already possessed unwilling humans, and they needed a vessel for the weapon, and they used Christina. Their intent was to keep her restrained, alive but unconscious. And then to destroy her when they accessed the weapon."

"But you rescued her."

"It didn't matter." Liam stood and moved to Mal's side. "She couldn't contain it. The power, the intensity. It was too much of a shock to her system. She started to lose control."

"I didn't know what else to do," Mal said. "My own powers weren't honed yet, and even if I had been able to absorb her energy, it was too far gone. And she was like us—I thought that the phoenix fire would regenerate her," he added, referring to the particular method by which the brotherhood was immortal. Death could take them, but it could not keep them, and they were rendered to ash in the phoenix flame, and then made mortal once again. "I thought that I could stop the weapon by stopping her," he explained. "I thought that she would come back to me."

He tried to shut out the memories. Him consoling her. Him promising to keep her safe, to keep the world safe.

And then that final, agonizing moment when he'd thrust his fire sword through her heart, and watched as life and blood spilled from her. He'd waited. Waited for the fire. Waited for her to come back to him so that they could start over. Soothing. Calming. Keeping her steady. Keeping her safe.

Except there was no fire. She didn't burn. She didn't regenerate.

She simply died.

And he was the one who had killed her.

He told Callie that, his stomach twisting as a single tear snaked down her cheek.

"We still don't understand why. The weapon, its energy. Somehow it kept her from being immortal. And I lost her. It was a long time before I found her again."

"Three-sixty-five AD," Liam said. "We were back in Egypt. And Mal sensed her presence."

"I didn't understand it," he said. "I'd believed she was lost for good. But I knew it was her. And I hoped. God help me, I hoped."

"She was reincarnated?"

"Essentially, yes."

"What happened?" Callie's words were a whisper.

"How well do you know Egyptian history?" Liam asked.

She shook her head.

"In the year 365, an earthquake leveled the Port of Alexandria. More than fifty-thousand people lost their lives."

Callie swallowed, then licked her lips.

"Christina?"

"She didn't know me," Mal said. "Didn't know herself." He drew in a breath with the memory. "I recognized her only by her essence. It was pure—undiluted—but she was in a new body, beautiful and yet unfamiliar. I went to her, and I hoped beyond reason." He dragged his fingers through his hair. "I didn't realize how far gone she was—how fucking impotent I was—until it was too late."

"It would have been worse if you hadn't acted when you did," Raine said quietly.

"Believe me," Mal said. "It was worse. And it just keeps happening over and over again. Her returning. Me killing."

"I'm so, so sorry," Callie said, then frowned.

"What?" Raine asked.

"Nothing. I was just wondering about before. I mean, she's an adult. So why didn't Mal become aware of her when she was a child?"

Mal shook his head. "I think that she is growing up in a new body, making a new life and new memories, and the weapon is growing along with her. I don't become aware until it has reached the point of being operational."

Callie nodded. "And we know it is operational," she said. "Because of what you felt tonight. And because of Egypt."

"Exactly. I wasn't as strong in Egypt," Mal said. "And she didn't remember. Things have changed. Everything has changed." He looked at Liam as he spoke, watched his friend shake his head slowly. "Dammit, Liam. I can help her fight it down. And if she remembers, she's going to be fighting, too. She's going to have something now to fight for."

"Like you do."

"Hell, yes," Mal said.

Liam scrubbed his hand over his jaw. "It's not just a question of control, Mal, and you damn well know it. The fuerie want her. They want to use her, and they will do whatever they can to reacquire her."

"Why do you think I have her under surveillance?"

"It's too dangerous and you know it. Our mission has always been to reacquire the weapon and either render it inert or get it the hell out of this dimension. And in case you've forgotten, we're stranded here. Until we find the final piece of the amulet, we have no power to bind the weapon or to get back across the void."

"The last time she manifested, we had only three of the seven amulets. Now we have six." He glanced at Callie and Raine. "We know the seventh exists—hell, we've touched it—and we are too close to end this now and send her back to death and waiting. Christ, Liam, it could be another century before I find her again."

"What is a century to us but a blink of an eye?" Liam asked.

"It's anguish without your mate beside you," Mal said harshly. "But you wouldn't know that."

Liam dragged his fingers through his hair, his eyes dark and tortured. "Do you think I don't understand? I do. And even though it's horrific, the truth is that a world without Christina is safe. We need the amulet first. Otherwise, with her alive, it's a catastrophe waiting to happen. Either because the fuerie grabs her and uses her, or because she's not strong enough to keep it down."

"She is. I'll make sure she is."

"Dammit, Mal—"

"No. You listen to me. She is strong, damn strong. Even after all these years, her essence hasn't dissipated. It's still her in there, fully and completely. Generation after generation, she has kept the core of Christina together. Even Livia couldn't manage that," he added, nodding toward Callie, who nodded.

"It's true," Raine said. "I can feel Livia within Cal, but some of her essence is in Oliver," he said, referring to Callie's father. "Some probably in other ancestors, some perhaps lost to the wind."

"That's the way it works in this dimension," Mal said to Liam, "and we both know it. Unless the essence is locked into form, it dissipates over time. And yet centuries have gone by without Christina having a form. Maybe she was able to keep herself together because of the weapon. Who knows? But what I do know is that she was able to fight her way back. To find her consciousness again. To draw on memories. And as far as I'm concerned, that makes her a hell of a lot stronger than you or me."

Liam exhaled. "Tell me exactly what you're suggesting."

"We bring her in. We protect her. I'm with her twenty-four/seven. She starts to lose control, I'm there to absorb it." His shoulders sagged. "Her stage name is Christina. She picked it without even knowing why. We've been on a hamster wheel for millennia," Mal pressed. "We owe her this, Liam. You know we do."

Slowly, Liam nodded. "If anything goes wrong, it will be my blade that strikes her down—and you, too, if you stand in the way. Whatever the risk. Whatever the cost."

"I should hope so," Mal said. "You've always had my back, Liam. I expect nothing less from you now."

CHAPTER 7

A S FAR AS I'm concerned, Saturday mornings mean sleeping late, drinking coffee with too much cream, tuning the television to cartoons, and kicking back with the newspaper and a bit of Bugs Bunny nostalgia.

Brayden, however, sees Saturdays slightly differently.

He's fine with the coffee and newspaper part of the equation, but as far as my best friend is concerned, Saturday morning cartoons do not mean stories filled with animated critters, Disney-fied cuteness, or Looney Tunes absurdity.

No, Brayden's idea of Saturday silliness

is the "ridiculous cartoon-like bullshit you see on all those reality shows. I mean seriously," he says to me as he navigates through all the shows that he has recorded off cable, "this is prime mindless entertainment."

How right he is.

We veg on the couch and channel-hop through what has to be the most extensive collection of reality television known to man.

"Do you watch nothing else?" I ask at one point, after we've bounced from a *Real Housewives of God Only Knows Where* to some new show about buying property in Alaska. Which looks pretty cool, actually, although I would never move that far north. Already I'm dreading the New York winter, and it's barely May.

"I am a connoisseur of television that requires neither thought nor commitment. I decided to see what all the fuss was about and rented *Game of Thrones* my first semester and got so addicted it's a wonder I didn't get booted out of med school. Now I watch only mindless fluff that I don't have to keep up with week to week."

"And there you go," I say. "The reason you're smart enough to be a doctor and I'm not." I bat my eyelashes at him. "I would have just given up television all together."

He narrows his eyes at me, obviously not certain if I'm praising him or insulting him. Finally, he settles for an affectionate "bitch" and hooks his arm around me as he kicks his feet up onto the coffee table.

As far as I can tell, the plan is to eat our way through the day. At least that's what it looks like to me, because Brayden went out earlier and returned with a bag of bagels, some cheese danish, a half-dozen blueberry muffins, and a tub full of whipped cream cheese that is approximately the size of a shoebox.

I'd given him grief at the time, but I'm now enthusiastically into the idea of carbohydrate overload. I've already finished a bagel, and am now picking at what is arguably the best blueberry muffin in the history of the universe. In fact, I'm about to suggest that we put in a call to Guinness World Records and have them investigate the muffin when I'm waylaid by the ring of the doorbell.

Since this is a security building, it has to be a resident or someone on staff, and I figure the least I can do to earn my keep around here is answer the door.

It's Clive who works part time at the security desk in the lobby. His sister's an aspiring actress, so we've spoken a few times since I've moved in. Now he hands me a fancy envelope made out of thick paper in a color that I figure would be called 'buff' in a stationery store. It's addressed to both Ms. Hart and Mr. Kline and the envelope is so fine and the calligraphy so precise that my first thought is that we've been invited to someone's wedding.

"What's that?" Brayden asks, as I take it back to the couch and start to slide my finger under the flap.

"Not sure, but it looks fancy. Which means I already know I have nothing to wear."

He holds out his hand just as I'm pulling a thick card out of the envelope. I pass it to him, then move in close so that I can look over his shoulder.

The owners and staff of Dark Pleasures invite you to visit us for drinks, appetizers, and conversation.

"Dark Pleasures?"

"It's a private club," Brayden says. "My dad's a member, but I don't think he ever goes, but that must be how they got my name."

"But how did they get mine?" It's weird, frankly. I'm not even officially a tenant yet, as Brayden hasn't gotten around to having the condo management add me to the mailbox or do any of the official new-roommate stuff.

"The invitation's for tonight at eight. We

should go," he says.

"I thought you had your study group tonight," I counter. I swore to myself when I moved in with him that I wasn't going to let the fact of my proximity mess with his studying. And that includes keeping him from doing stupid things like going to fancy clubs when he's supposed to be studying gross anatomy or brains or dissecting a cadaver or something equally doctorish.

"All the more reason to go tonight. We get to scope it out, but the commitment is limited. So if they try to get us to join up and fork over some exorbitant membership fee, we can honestly say that we have another engagement and will have to get back to them. Come on," he presses. "The timing couldn't be more perfect. And if nothing else, I bet the drinks are first rate."

I flop back down on his sofa and pull my knees up to my chest. "I don't know." I'm feeling oddly reticent, which is weird because going to a private club is about as New York as it gets, and didn't I come here wanting the full Manhattan experience?

Brayden aims narrowed eyes at me. "What's with you?"

"Nothing." My voice comes out just a little too earnest. "I just figured it was a day to laze about in pajamas."

"Oh, please. We have the entire day left to veg, so you won't miss out on the lazy Saturday experience, and I still owe you drinks from Thursday."

"It's just a scam," I say. "They want to lure you in, treat you nice, and try to convince you that you really need to join. That belonging to Dark Pleasures is the secret handshake that will make your medical career."

"When you put it like that, maybe I should join. If there's even an off chance that I'll learn the secret handshake..."

He trails off with a grin. I just roll my eyes.

"Oh, come on. Who cares if it's a sales pitch. One night of free drinks and appetizers? Besides, the building's awesome. It's been around since the mid-nineteenth century and I've always wanted to go inside. It's just a few blocks away on 63rd Street."

I open my mouth to protest again, but I feel stupid putting my foot down like this, especially since I can't explain—not even to myself—why I'm so damn hesitant. "Fine," I say. "But in that case, we're not lazing around today. If you're going to drag me to some hoity-toity private club, I'm going to drag you shopping."

For a minute, I think that may be enough to make him back off the plan. Brayden has a rich boy's fashion sense, but he'd rather take a bullet than brave a department store. But then he cocks his head. "Lunch while we're out?"

"Indian food?"

He thrusts his hand out. "Deal."

And as I put my hand in his, I can't shake the weird sensation that I have just taken a giant step. But toward what, I have no idea.

"Not bad," Brayden says as we stand on the sidewalk in front of 36 East 63rd Street.

I turn my attention from the five-story building and focus on my friend. "Understatement much?" I'd thought that Brayden's building was amazing, and it is. Sleek and modern, it reaches majestically to the heavens, the walls of glass providing residents with exceptional views of the city.

But compared to Number 36, Brayden's building is cold and austere. A snooty bitch rather than a welcoming friend. Because despite being accessible only to members, there is no denying that the entrance to Dark Pleasures is as inviting as it is elegant, as if it is reaching out from a different age when the business of society was, in fact, to be social.

The building is only five stories tall, and though it is shaped mostly like a box, the first two floors are convex, making it look a bit like a building with the tower at the base instead of the top. The mix of red brick and off-white plaster adds to the impression that the building is an elegant antique trapped in a modern city.

But what I find most interesting is that the building is actually set away from the sidewalk in a way that manages to be inviting even while making clear to passers-by that it is an exclusive venue not meant for the general public.

I have my hand on the black iron fence that surrounds the property. Five steps lead down to a courtyard and then to the heavy wooden door that marks the building's entrance. I glance at Brayden, then start down the stairs. "Here goes nothing."

He paces me, and we reach the courtyard together. As I'd expected, it really is like entering another world. Even the air seems cleaner and more fragrant, probably courtesy of the flowers and plants placed decoratively around the enclosed area.

The focal point of the polished, wooden door is a gold knocker in the shape of a bird.

It is mounted at eye level and its trailing tail feathers act as a handle. I look to Brayden, then shrug as I reach for it.

Before I actually knock, Brayden says, "Look." He's nodding toward a brass plaque that is mounted just to the right of the door. I lean over and read it:

Dark Pleasures

Est. 1895

Members Only

"Guess we're in the right place," I say, then use the metal tail feathers to rap soundly on the door.

After a moment, the door opens to reveal an elderly man. He has neatly combed white hair, perfectly pressed livery, and a don't-fuck-with-me attitude. Naturally, I assume he is the butler.

"Um." I'm about to expand upon that auspicious conversational opener when he sniffs lightly.

"Ms. Hart. Mr. Kline."

I look to Brayden, who shrugs. Apparently the staff at really exclusive private clubs are expected to identify potential members on sight.

I'm trying to decide if that's really great customer service or just a little creepy when the butler inclines his head. "Welcome to Dark Pleasures. If you'd please follow me…"

Since there is no rational reason for me to feel so jittery, I resist the urge to take Brayden's hand. Instead, I make do with meeting his eyes as we step over the threshold and into a dark wood-paneled foyer. Like the exterior suggested, the walls of this room are curved. Other than that architectural feature, though, there is nothing about the room itself that is particularly extraordinary. That honor is reserved to the contents of the room. Specifically, to an enormous glass bowl filled with what appears to be living, breathing fire.

I gasp and move toward it, compelled to

take a closer look. The bowl sits atop a marble pedestal in the center of the foyer. Now that I am beside it—close enough that I could reach my hand into the flames—I see that the bowl is filled not with wood or some other fuel, but with red and blue glass pebbles.

I hug myself, squeezing tight to ward off a sudden flood of nervous energy even as Brayden moves to stand beside me.

"That's pretty cool," he says. He bends down and looks at it from underneath. "Is there a gas line running up the column?"

The butler's brows rise slightly, but he says only, "That centerpiece is one of the treasures of the house. Please, follow me."

The butler continues toward a set of double doors on the opposite side of the foyer. As I fall in step behind him, Brayden shoots me the quirky grin that I know so well—the one that suggests we are setting off on a great adventure. When we were kids, that look used to fill me with a sense of wondrous glee as we would go off to explore the vacant lots and empty houses in the growing subdivision where we lived.

Now, it is not glee that floods me but an oppressive sense of foreboding accompanied by the strange, unwelcome sensation that I am moving inexorably toward the one thing in all the world that has the power to destroy me.

"Jaynie?"

Brayden's hand brushes my shoulder and I let out a yelp so loud it rips me from my reverie. "Sorry!" I take a deep breath. I am completely mortified, all the more so when I see the way the butler is looking at me, as if I am something unpleasant that a guest tracked in on the sole of his shoe. "I—I was thinking about that bowl. You just startled me. Sorry." I say the last with a thin smile that I hope looks properly contrite.

It seems to satisfy the butler. Brayden, however, knows me too well. "Are you okay?" His eyes are on me and he speaks with such precision that I know he is worried. That's fair, I suppose. I'm a little worried myself.

"I'm fine," I say firmly. "I was imagining what this place may have been like back in the day. Just trying to picture it back then. And I was lost in thought when you touched me." I reach for his hand and squeeze his fingers. "Really. I'm fine."

"Then it wasn't—"

"Just imagination," I assure him, and to my relief, he seems to believe the lie.

In front of us, the butler waits beside the doors, his expression entirely unreadable. "Shall we continue?"

I hesitate, because this is my chance to turn back. I can make up some excuse and return to the apartment, leaving Brayden to either go with me or continue on. He would be perturbed, but he'd get over it. And I would be free of these oppressive walls and the fear that I do not have the strength to survive whatever journey I am on.

But the truth is that I don't want to run. I want to go forward and come out the other side, and then I want to look back and thrust out my middle finger and say "fuck you" to all the fears and fugues that have plagued my whole, goddamn life.

"Yes," I say firmly. "We should absolutely go on."

If either of the men I'm with understand the magnitude of the statement I've just made, they don't show it. Instead, the butler simply puts a card key against the door, then pushes it open to reveal a lounge area full of wood and leather and the subtle, spicy scent of cigar smoke.

The lounge is like something out of an old movie, and I've never been in a room that feels so rich. Not just in terms of the collective net worth that must be represented here, but in the deep sensuality of the leather and the wood. In the straight, classic lines of the humidor that runs perpendicular to a long, polished bar that I think must be made of mahogany. In the crystal glasses that gleam from behind the bar, and in the array of well-aged bottles of scotch that line the glass shelves, glittering and shining in the room's muted lighting.

All around us, people laugh and talk, their voices mixing with the soft, classical music that fills the air. Scent and sound merge to create a magic carpet of sensuality that I think could whisk me away to another world if only I would let it.

I try to look around—to fully take in my surroundings—but my attention keeps returning to the bar. Not to the liquor, but to two men who are seated there. One sits with his back to us, facing the bar, his reflection in the bar mirror hidden by a selection of fine whiskeys. But though I can see little of him, he is undeniably familiar to me. I feel as though I could close my eyes and trace the line of his shoulders under his suit jacket. And I can imagine the way his coal-dark hair would feel if it brushed lightly over my fingers the same way that it brushes the back of his collar.

He is relaxed—a man probably having a drink with a friend—and yet even in this casual moment there is something about him that suggests power and confidence and grace. I want to go to him. Hell, I want to touch him, and the intensity of that desire scares me, because I have never felt such a strong familiarity to another person, let alone a man I do not even know.

But you do know him.

I shiver in defense against the unexpected thought, and feel a rush of gratitude when Brayden brushes his fingers against my arm and distracts me. "Look," he whispers.

I glance at my friend's face, then realize that he is also watching the two men. His attention, however, has been drawn to the second one, who is sitting at more of an angle, so that I can actually see most of his face. It's exceptional, but what surprises me is the tattoo that I see extending up his neck, suggesting that there is more ink beneath his shirt. And when he reaches for a glass on the bar, the cuff of his shirt shifts back just enough for me to see the edge of a tat decorating his wrist.

I catch Brayden's eye and he leans over

to whisper, "Maybe the place isn't as stuffy as it seems." I have to agree. For that matter, I don't think anything about this place is what it seems.

Beside us, the butler is speaking to a young brunette who is seated at a small antique desk just inside the doors. "Ms. Hart and Mr. Kline are prospective members."

"Thank you, Mr. Daley," she says, standing. She projects competence and efficiency, and matches those attributes with a welcoming smile. "I'll take good care of them."

Our escort inclines his head, and then leaves the way we came in. I'm sorry to see him go, because now we are here, and I'm still not entirely sure where "here" is. And I'm certainly not sure why I've been invited.

"I'm Tanya," the girl says. "Why don't I show you around?"

"I'll take care of that, Tanya."

The voice comes from behind, but I know that it is him before I even turn around. *The man from the bar.* Not the one with tattoos, but the other one. The familiar one. I know because of the way my skin prickles. Because of the heat that seems to buzz in the air.

And when I do turn around to face him—when I see that it is not Tanya who has his attention but me—I know that I am not the only one who feels the explosion that is building between us.

"Of course, Mr. Greer." Tanya smiles at him, then nods to Brayden and me before returning to her desk. And in that moment, the spell breaks, and when Mr. Greer turns his attention to Brayden and holds out his hand, I am starting to doubt that I'd felt anything odd at all.

"I'm Malcolm Greer," he says, shaking Brayden's hand as he smiles at both of us. "I'm one of the owners of Dark Pleasures."

Malcolm. That name again, just as it had whispered through my mind at the theater. And those eyes—oh, Christ, he has the storm gray eyes of the man from my dream.

"Thank you for the invitation," Brayden

is saying.

I say nothing—instead, I am staring at Malcolm Greer, wondering who he is and why I seem to feel him so strongly. Why I know his name. His eyes.

Thinking that we should never have come here tonight, because he is a man I could fall for, and I don't want to fall for any man. Worrying that something is happening here that I don't understand, something that I should know, but somehow can't remember.

And I'm suddenly cold and just a little afraid, because I am my mother's daughter, and I don't want to be like her, living in a world of fantasies and conspiracies and shadows, always afraid that—

"Ms. Hart?" I hear the concern in Malcolm's voice, and snap back to myself.

"Yes," I blurt. "Sorry."

I take a deep breath and will myself to breathe slowly. To calm down. I'm being absurd, and I know it. The man is familiar; so what? He's so damn good looking he probably reminds me of a celebrity. And as for that name—well, that is obviously just a coincidence. It's not that unusual a name, after all.

"Jay? Are you okay?"

"Of course," I say. "Just light headed." I turn my attention back to Malcolm. "And I also want to thank you for the invitation. Although I suppose I owe Brayden thanks, too. I mean, when you get right down to it, he's the real reason I'm here." I realize as soon as I've spoken that it's a stupid thing to say. Typical, though, as I babble when I get nervous. And Malcolm Greer makes me very nervous.

Right now, he's looking at me with such an odd expression, that I feel even more foolish.

"Ms. Hart," he says, with a strange little smile. "I believe you have it backwards. Mr. Kline is here because of you."

CHAPTER 8

"M E?" I LAUGH, then glance at Brayden. Like me, he looks as if he's expecting a punch line.

"You," Malcolm says. His voice is flat, but I see what I think is humor in his eyes. "Is that so hard to believe?"

"Honestly? Yes." I look around the room, now even more edgy than I'd been before. He must be teasing me—lord knows there's no reason that I would be on the radar of an exclusive private club. But all that does is underscore the strange sensation that I know this man from somewhere. And since I'm drawing a blank, my discomfort is climbing.

I clear my throat. "So, um, if you're trying to recruit us, shouldn't you at least offer us a drink?"

He hesitates, and for a moment I think that he's going to apologize or offer an explanation or say something that sets me at ease. But all he does is incline his head and then indicate a nearby table. "Please," he says, this time bringing Bray back into the conversation.

As we walk the short distance to the table, I admire his lean, athletic frame that seems made for the fine, tailored suit he wears. He pulls out a chair for me, which is a good decision on his part, as it knocks my irritation down a notch. I've always been a sucker for a man with good manners.

I settle into my chair at this intimate round table, and as I do, I take the opportunity to study his face, with its sculptured, classic features that manage to be both elegant and ruggedly masculine. I want to reach out and touch him, the urge so powerful that I press my palms to the armrests in order to keep them in place.

But there is no saving me from his eyes. I've fallen into them. Those storm gray eyes that I am so certain I have seen before, even if only in my dreams. He holds my gaze for what must be only seconds but seems like millennia, and I let the tempest take me, a wild, passionate heat that holds the promise of danger and excitement—and so much more, too. I don't understand it, and yet I crave it. And I feel as though I could stay this way forever, Brayden and the world and everyone at Dark Pleasures be damned.

Then he lifts his hand to signal the waitress, and the spell is broken. I feel a blush creep up my neck, because even though we didn't touch at all, I can't shake the feeling that we have just shared something deeply intimate.

A college-aged waiter arrives, and Malcolm orders a plate of artisan cheeses along with three glasses of The Macallan 18 year scotch, straight up for him and Brayden, on the rocks for me.

I cock my head. "How did you know I like it over ice? For that matter, how did you know I like scotch?"

"Would you believe I guessed?"

"No," I say as Bray laughs.

Mal joins him. "I take it from your reaction that I guessed right?"

"You did," Bray says. "And she's impressed."

"Good." Malcolm leans back in his chair, looking entirely at ease and completely in control. "My goal is to impress both of you." He's a tall man, and as he stretches his legs out, his ankle brushes against my calf, setting off a storm of sensation that is out of proportion with the casual nature of the touch.

"I'm quite impressed so far," Brayden says as he turns his head to look at the stunning architecture and furnishings. "This place is incredible." He's fallen into the corporate-like politeness that I know he learned from summers in Manhattan with his father, and which served him so well during med school interviews.

"I can do better," Malcolm says as he lifts a hand to wave at someone across the room. "Dagny. Come join us."

I turn to follow his gaze and see an absolutely stunning woman with a mass of auburn curls pinned up so that tendrils fall with casual elegance. She's slim and wears a white sheath dress with matching white shoes, and I can't help but think that she looks like a candle, tall and slender with a crown of flame.

She flashes a brilliant smile toward Malcolm, and I feel an unpleasant twist in my gut. I tell myself it can't possibly be jealousy—I barely know Mal, after all—but of course that's exactly what it is. I force myself to smile politely as she approaches, then dig my fingernails into the armrests of my chair as she perches lightly on the armrest of his, right between him and Brayden.

"Hi," she says, leaning forward and extending her hand to me. "I'm Dagny. You must be Christina."

"Jaynie," I correct.

"Oh." She glances quickly at Mal, the question plain on her face.

"I'm afraid I used your stage name when I mentioned that you and Brayden were coming. I hope you don't mind."

"Not at all." I'm trying out that overly polite thing myself, but the truth is that I'd much rather be Jaynie around this man. Somehow, that just seems safer.

I smile brightly at Dagny. "So tell me, is that how it works? All the members learn about the new blood?"

"Not all the members," Dagny assures me. "Only the VIPs." She seems so genuine and so sweet that I like her despite the fact that she's now resting one hand on Mal's shoulder in order to keep her balance on the thin armrest. But that bit of familiarity is counterbalanced by the fact that she's otherwise not paying attention to Mal at all. Instead, she's entirely focused on Brayden.

And from what I'm seeing, Brayden has

noticed that, too.

"I'm Brayden," he says, then holds her offered hand for what I calculate is at least five seconds too long.

"I know." Her smile is bright and just a little mischievous, and when the waiter returns with our drinks, she takes one of the glasses with no ice and helps herself to a small sip. "You don't mind, do you?"

"Nope," Brayden says. I see the heat rise in my best friend's eyes, and as I take a sip from my own glass I can't help but wonder if I'll be bumping into Dagny when I stumble into the kitchen to get coffee in the morning.

"Good." Her eyes never leave his as she downs the rest of his drink, then eases off of Mal's chair to stand beside Bray. She holds her hand out to him. "Looks like you need a refill."

"I guess I do." And then—because he is my best friend in the entire world, he meets my eyes, unwilling to leave unless he's certain I'll be okay. "Do you mind if I take

Dagny to the bar and buy her a drink?"

For the briefest of moments I want to beg Bray to stay by my side. Because there is something about Malcolm Greer that both compels me and terrifies me.

Mostly, though, he excites me. And it has been a long time since any man stirred such a variety of emotions within me.

"Yeah," I finally say as I turn to look at the man beside me. "Yeah, I'll be just fine."

Bray rises with an eagerness I rarely see in him where women are concerned, and I watch as he presses his hand lightly to the base of Dagny's spine as he guides her through the crowd to the bar.

"Ah, those crazy kids," I say, and Mal laughs.

"I thought Dagny might enjoy meeting him. She's just moved back to New York from Los Angeles."

"What does she do?"

"She works for me."

"Oh," I say. "And what do you do?"

He says nothing. Instead, he reaches for

his glass and takes a long drink of his scotch, and all the while his eyes never leave my face. "Is that what we're going to do now? Casual small talk?"

His low voice fills my senses like music, threatening to sweep me away. "I—" I swallow and try again. "Do you want an honest answer?"

"I have no use for a dishonest one."

"In that case, yes. Small talk. The weather is always a good choice."

A muscle in his jaw twitches, and I can't tell if he's amused or frustrated. "Politics? Religion?"

"Don't be absurd."

"Hollywood?"

I tilt my head from side to side as I consider. "Possibly. It has the potential to get too personal."

His brows lift. "As in whether you prefer network or cable? PG or NC-17?"

I feel my cheeks heat. "Something like that."

"Witty banter?"

"Definitely off-limits," I say.

"Mmm." He steeples his hands on the table. "I can see your point. Banter with you might inspire more sexual innuendoes than are usually tolerated among polite society."

His voice has taken on a rough, sensual edge, and as a shiver runs down my spine, I try to tilt my head down. I don't want him to see my face, because the mere thought of Malcolm Greer anywhere close to sexual innuendoes is more than I can handle at the moment.

He, however, takes no pity on me. Instead, he reaches forward and tilts my chin up so that I have no choice but to look into those fathomless eyes.

"Malcolm." My whisper is like a plea, and he releases me. He remains as he is, though, leaning forward, his elbows on the table, his eyes fixed on mine. And when he speaks, his voice is so soft and gentle it makes me want to cry. "Tell me, Christina. What are you afraid of."

I blink, and am mortified when a tear

trickles down my cheek. "My name is Jaynie."

He shakes his head, his mouth quirking up in an ironic smile. "No. With me, you will always be Christina."

I close my eyes and take a deep breath, trying to gather myself. "I don't understand any of this." It is probably the most honest thing I've said since we arrived.

"What? Tell me specifically what you don't understand."

I open my mouth, though I have no idea what I intend to say. Somehow, "every-thing" seems far too broad.

I am saved from having to find words by the arrival of our cheese plate. "Thanks for ordering this."

"You said you were feeling light-headed. I thought it might be hunger."

This time when I smile, it is entirely genuine. "You were right, actually. Bray and I were going to grab something to eat when we went out shopping, but we got so caught up there wasn't time. He grabbed a sandwich at the apartment, but I only grabbed a shower."

"I'm sorry you went hungry, but if you made the sacrifice to buy the outfit you're wearing, then I have to say it was worth it. You look stunning."

"I'm glad you like it." My words are soft, but they are heartfelt. I'd fallen in love with the dress the moment I tried it on. It's black and the material is so light and soft it feels as though I'm wearing a cloud. The bodice is fitted, and cut low enough that it puts my rather average cleavage to good advantage. It has short, flirty sleeves, and a skirt that hits just above my knees and has a sassy little swing when I walk.

I've never felt particularly sexy, but in this dress I think I could go sit at a bar and attract the attention of every male in the room. And though I'd bought it with no particular man in mind, I cannot deny that the way Malcolm looks at me now is making the torment I put my credit card through very, very worth it.

"Malcolm ..." His name tastes delicious on my tongue.

He reaches across the table and takes my hand, and it feels like the most natural thing in the world. "You can call me Mal," he says. "Though I do love the way you say my full name."

"Mal," I repeat, and then realize that I've been calling him that in my head on and off the whole evening. "That suits you, too."

"What did you want to ask?"

I blink at him. "What do you mean?"

"You said my name. I assumed a question was going to follow."

"Oh." Once again, I blush. Frankly, I think I've broken some sort of blushing record this evening. "No. I—I just wanted to say it."

"Did you?"

I can hear the heat in his voice. More than that, I can feel it. It winds through me, warming my blood and settling in all sorts of interesting places. My lips. My breasts. Between my thighs.

I realize that I am about to moan and gently tug my hand away.

"Now you're being cruel," he says.

"Just careful."

"I didn't realize hands were so dangerous."

"With you, I think that words are equally so."

His wide, sensual mouth curves into a grin. "Well, look at us. We've moved from small talk to witty banter after all. Shall I alert the media?"

I can't help it—I laugh. "Can I ask you a question?"

"Anything."

"Have we met before?"

He hesitates, then lifts his hand. And though I realize that he is only signaling the waiter for more drinks, it seems to me that he is stalling. "What makes you think that?" he finally asks.

"I don't know. Nothing specific. You just seem familiar."

"Maybe I just have one of those faces."

I roll my eyes. "Hardly."

"Perhaps you know me from the thea-ter."

"The theater?"

"Story Street. I invested recently."

I sit up straighter. This is starting to make sense. "Where you there on Friday? Watching rehearsal?"

He nods, and the pieces fall into place. I must have heard his name whispered among the staff. And as for the sensation that he seemed familiar—well, maybe that was just my subconscious pointing out an attractive guy.

Voila. Mystery solved.

"Is that why you say the invitation was because of me?"

Mal doesn't answer, but I see the small smile and feel even more vindicated.

Across the room, I see Bray signal for me to come over. He's alone, and since that seems odd under the circumstances, I tell Mal not to go away and head over to him.

"I'm gonna book," he says.

"You're leaving? What about Dagny?"

He grins. "She's pretty great, right? She made me swear I'd come back tomorrow. Apparently this trial membership thing is good for two weeks."

"Okay, I give up. Why are you leaving if she likes you?"

"Call me crazy, but I actually want to be a doctor someday. And while I'm pretty sure that I could convince Dagny to *play* doctor with me—"

"Fine, fine, I get it. Study group. I forgot." I swallow my disappointment at cutting the evening short. "Let me just say goodbye and I'll be right back."

"Oh, please. Why should you leave when all I'd do is dump you at home and then head to the lab? Especially when you seem to be getting on so well."

"I like him."

His brows lift. "This is an interesting development. So maybe I don't need to remind you that you have to jiggle the button on the coffee grinder to get it to work. You might be getting your coffee here in the morning."

"No way," I say.

"Bullshit."

"I'm not looking for a relationship." Since I've never looked for a relationship, my statement is absolutely accurate.

"Doesn't mean you can't fuck him."

I shrug. "Maybe. We'll see."

He studies my face. "You don't want to get involved with him, and yet you don't want to just roll around with him. My darling Jay, I think this qualifies as an honest-to-goodness conundrum."

I give him a shove. "Go," I say. "Go now."

He catches me by the wrists and pulls me in for a hug. "Whatever you do, be smart. And if you come home, take a taxi or have Malcolm walk you. Okay?"

"Promise," I say, because I've watched enough episodes of *Law & Order* to know that walking around Manhattan by yourself after dark is a recipe for disaster.

I head back to Mal, and have to force myself to walk slowly so that I don't look too eager. Or, worse, so that I don't trip in my heels.

His smile when I take my seat is as potent as if I'd returned from a long journey across the sea.

"I'm glad you're back," he says guilelessly. "I don't like it when you're away from me."

"Are you always this direct?" I ask, though I cannot deny the warm surge of pleasure that flows through me.

"Only about things that are important to me." His words are like a caress, stroking and teasing me, making my skin prickle and my heart flutter in my chest.

"Oh." I swallow, then bite the bullet. "Am I important to you?"

"Very."

I meet his eyes. "Why?"

He reaches across the table and takes my hands in his. His are warm and large, and I cannot help but gasp from the force of the connection that seems to surge between us, as if this slight contact has completed a circuit, and we are both now lit up. "Why are you fighting me?"

His words are gentle, but they strike me with all the force of a slap. I tug my hands away and put them in my lap. "I didn't know that I was." I stand up. Then I feel foolish and sit down again. But I'm edgy, and I can't help but shift in my chair.

The truth is that I was fighting him. I know that I'm important to him. I know that he likes my company. And yet I cannot simply succumb and see where it leads. I have to analyze. I have to weigh and balance and try to control every little thing, because if I don't, something might sneak in through a crack and hurt me when I least expect it.

I stand again, my thoughts too wild and jarring to let me stay still.

"Do you want to walk?" There is no frustration in his voice. If there had been, I think I would have just told him good night.

Instead, I nod. "Thanks. Yes." I draw a

breath as common sense returns. "Actually, it's getting late. Maybe you could walk me home?"

I see the disappointment in his eyes, but to his credit, he only nods. "It would be my pleasure."

We leave through a different door, this one in the back past the humidors. As we walk, he puts his hand at the base of my spine the same way that Bray led Dagny. The connection is undeniably intimate, and I sigh with pleasure at the surge of warmth that spreads down my back and between my thighs. Maybe I'm not going to fuck him, but I can't deny that I like the way he makes me feel.

As we're exiting, we pass a tall man with copper hair and piercing blue eyes that are focused very intently on my face. Once the door into the lounge has closed behind him, I turn back, as if I will see some lingering evidence of why he seemed so interested in me. Of course there is none.

Beside me, Mal has come to a stop. We

are in a large room that appears to have once been part of a ballroom before this brownstone was redesigned. "Tell me something," he says. "Why did you suddenly want to leave?"

I shrug. "It's getting late, that's all." Once again I turn toward the door from which we've just exited, only this time I'm trying to change the subject. "Who was that? The man we passed?"

"Asher," he says, as if that explains everything.

"Why was he looking at me like that?"

"Like what?"

"As if he knew me. As if he didn't trust me."

Mal brushes my cheek. "I doubt that. More likely, he was admiring you."

It's not the truth, but I don't call him on the lie because I'm enjoying this time with him, and I don't want to spoil it because of an enigmatic look from a man I don't even know.

As we step further into the room, I see a

small, old-fashioned elevator. "Are there apartments above the club? Do you live here?"

"There are a few apartments," he says. "But no, I don't live on site, though a few of the brotherhood do."

"The brotherhood?" He's leading me across the tile floor away from the elevator and toward a side door.

"Think of it as a partnership. We own the building and run the club."

"Oh. I'm impressed," I say, and I mean it. What I have seen of both the building and the club are exceptional. Both well-kept, well-run, and overflowing with taste.

"Are you going to answer me?" he asks as he holds the door open.

I step past him into the humid night air. "Was there a question?" We're in a small courtyard that connects this building with the one next to it. And though I can see little of it other than than its brick facade, I have the impression that it is at least as old and elegant as number 36.

He takes my elbow. "Yes, there was a question. But I'll rephrase it. Why are you running from me?"

I look at him. "I'm not. I swear. Just the opposite, really. With anybody else, I would have been long gone by now."

He seems to study my face, and I have to force myself not to look away, because I am certain that he sees more than I want to reveal. "Why?"

I shrug. "I don't usually talk like this with other people. I hold things in. About the only time I don't hold back is on stage, but then I'm someone else."

"I thought you didn't like small talk."

"I don't. Usually I just don't talk at all."

He chuckles. "And yet here you are with me, having a lovely conversation. Why do you think that is?"

"It's not me," I say, unable to control the breathy quality of my voice. "So it must be you."

"Fair enough. Why?"

"Something about you."

"What?" He takes a step closer.

I take a step back and shake my head. "I don't know."

"I do." He takes another step, and though I try to maintain the distance between us, I no longer can. Somehow he has eased us up against the side of the second building. We're beside the service door, and I feel the bite of rough brick against my shoulders.

I want to speak, but I seem to have forgotten how. And so I can only look at him, my heart pounding in my chest, my nerves on fire. And yet at the same time, this feels so perfect. So right. And I do not know if I want to fling myself into his arms or run away as far and as fast as I can manage.

"Do you know how the world works, Christina?"

"What do you mean?"

"Not the earth, but the entire of the universe. Time is a relative thing, and matter can be manipulated. But a person's essence—their energy, their soul—that is the only real truth in the universe."

I shake my head and tell myself I don't know what he's talking about. And that's true. I don't. But I can't deny that his words make me uncomfortable. As if I were to hold them close and polish them to a mirror-shine, I'd see myself reflected back in them.

"Don't deny it," he continues. "You understand me. Hell, you *know* me. Maybe not this flesh, but your essence. The core of you. You've known me from the first moment you saw me."

I lick my lips as a vague panic rises in me. "I think you're confusing me with my mother. She was the one who was in to all that woo-woo past life bullshit."

"And you're not?"

"My mom was a nutcase." I speak firmly and emphasize every word. "I'm nothing like her."

"There's nothing crazy about the truth, Christina." He brushes my cheek with the pad of his thumb, the contact so soothing I want to close my eyes and get lost in it. "And whatever the source, you're attracted to me. Don't fight it. Why would you want to? This spark, this connection. It's not something to run from. It's something to foster. To build. To grow.

"Christina," he continues, and I can hear the tension in his voice, as if he's fighting for control. He moves his thumb, now brushing my lower lip. "Please. Don't fight me. Hell, don't fight *us*."

I draw in a stuttering breath. "You're— you're very direct."

"I am. Would you like me to be more direct?"

"I'm not sure."

"I want you, Christina. In my mind, I already have you."

"Oh." I shiver as wave of pleasure crests over me. "What exactly does that mean?"

His mouth curves into the kind of smile that suggests long nights in a warm bed. "So many things. Mostly it means that you're mine to touch. To tease. To pleasure." His palm cups my breast and I gasp as his thumb flicks over my nipple. "Do you know how many ways there are to please a woman? Do you know how much delight can be wrought with nothing more than a fingertip?"

I make a small whimpering sound, my body quivering with longing.

"I will show you, Christina. That, and so much more."

His voice drops to a low, raw whisper that seems to brush my skin with the same sensuality as his touch. "I want to take you to heights you haven't imagined, go with you to places we could never go before. I want to bind you so that you have no defense against the onslaught of passion, so that you have no choice but to trust me and submit to me. And I want to take you to the edge and back."

He trails his fingertip over my jawline, and I am already so aroused by his words, that I almost come from that seemingly innocent touch.

"I'm going to fuck you, Christina. But more than that, lover, I'm going to enjoy you. I'm going to please you. And I'm going to make love to you until we have made up for all the lost years and all the missing moments."

Heat builds in his eyes as he leans toward me. I tense, expecting his touch and wanting his kiss, then exhale in surprise and disappointment when I realize that he is using a key card to open the door next to us.

I swallow. "I thought you were walking me home."

"I was. My home."

I start to protest, but he presses his finger over my lips.

"I told you, Christina. I want you."

"Do you always get what you want?"

He hesitates only briefly, then shakes his head. "No, not always. But I couldn't bear not to get you." He gestures to the now-open door. "Will you come in with me?"

"I want to," I admit. "And that's not something I would expect to hear myself say."

"In that case, I'm honored."

"You have a very strange effect on me."

"Do I?" His mouth curves with amusement. "I think I like the sound of that."

"I'm not so sure that I do," I say honestly.

"Don't do that." He cups my chin, his voice earnest. "Don't fear what's between us."

I drag my teeth over my lower lip, even as I dig deep for courage. "I don't understand it," I admit. "But I like it."

And then, before I can stop myself, I raise myself up on my toes, hold on to his shoulders, and capture his mouth in a kiss.

He responds immediately, turning my already wild kiss even more passionate. He captures me with his mouth even while taking my hands in his and stretching them up so that I am flat against the wall, and he is pressed flat against me. Long and hard, and I can feel the press of his erection against my stomach and—oh, dear god—I want more. Everything. *Him.*

"Christina." My name on his lips is as sensual as a caress, as wild as a seduction, and I feel my body opening to him. My breasts hot and heavy, my thighs tingling in anticipation of his touch. And my sex—oh, yes, please. I want to feel him touch me. Stroke me.

I want to get lost to the power of his touch. I want to feel him moving inside me.

And, yes, I want to explode in his arms.

He shifts my wrists so that he can hold my arms up with only one hand. With his right hand now free, he trails his fingers down my body even as his mouth explores my ear, my neck, all sorts of new and enticing erogenous zones that make me tremble with longing. And then his fingers are at my waist. My hip. My thigh.

Now they are rising, higher and higher along the soft skin of my thigh, the thin fabric of my skirt rising with each motion, and my sex throbbing with anticipation of his certain touch.

"Not here," he murmurs. "Not again. But I have to have you. Please, Christina. Come inside with me."

Yes, yes.

I want to shout the word. Just the thought of Mal, hot and naked and hard against me is enough to make me abandon everything I know, everything I am. To make me forget everything I've feared.

Except.

I draw in a breath, my body cooling a bit as I force myself to ease back. To *think*, dammit.

Because what would come next?

If I sleep with Mal, what could possibly come next?

I know that the sex will be amazing, but I don't just want sex. I'll get tangled up with him. He will fill me. He'll consume me.

And then, he will break my heart.

I know it as certainly as I draw breath. And so, with infinite regret, I turn my head away from his kisses and shift my stance to close my legs.

"Lover, no…"

The endearment makes me shiver—and almost makes me change my mind. But I hold fast to my decision. "I'm sorry. I—I just can't. Not now."

"Christina."

I shake my head then look up at his face. "It hurts too much."

I see confusion in his eyes. "What does?"

"The end, Malcolm. I already know I won't be able to bear it when it ends."

CHAPTER 9

"WHO'S WATCHING HER?" Liam asked.

"I should be," Mal said. "God*dammit.*" He slammed his fist down at the table, causing Liam and Raine to exchange mild glances. They were in the VIP room, sitting around one of the larger tables they often used for planning missions. Mal and Liam, along with Raine, Jessica, and even Asher, who'd met with Liam earlier in the day for a debrief and was now sitting quietly, soaking up the conversation as he usually did. Asher was quiet, but sharp, and when he spoke, the other members of the brotherhood listened.

That was one of the reasons he'd been

named Second and stood ready to replace either Liam or Mal as leader should either of them resign the position or become unable to carry out their duties.

Right now, he was sitting impassively in the wake of Mal's outburst.

"Fuck," Mal said as he pressed his fingertips to his temple, wishing he could just pull the pain and frustration out of him like a string.

"Mal," Jessica said soothingly. "Give her time. She's coming at this from a completely different place than you are."

"Do you think I don't get that?" he snapped, then immediately regretted his temper. "I'm sorry, Jessica. I'm an asshole tonight."

She flashed a pert smile. "And that's different from every other night how?"

Mal shot a glance toward Liam. "Can't you control your wife?"

"Can't you control yours?"

Mal winced. "Apparently not." He ran his fingers through his hair. "She said that she can't bear it when it ends. Why would she say that?"

"You know why," Raine said, and Mal had to nod. Of course *he* knew why. It was Christina who didn't understand the wellspring of her fears. And yet her subconscious clearly did understand. Deep inside, Christina believed that what was between them would end because that's what had happened before.

Because Mal had ended it over and over and over again—had ended *her*—for three thousand years.

Christ, after all that, she'd probably worked up one hell of a grudge.

"Look, man," Liam said. "I know it's hard. But right now I need to know who's watching her."

"Dante." Raine said. "He sent Dante."

Liam's eyes sharpened. "Did Dante detect that there were fuerie around?"

"No fuerie," Mal said. "Not now. But I needed to send someone to keep an eye on her, and he was the best choice available."

Raine made a derisive sound, but otherwise said nothing. Mal knew why he was irritated; both Raine and Dante had been in the VIP lounge when Mal had burst in, saying that he needed a tail on Christina right then.

Raine had volunteered—and Mal had ignored him and assigned Dante. Now he looked at Raine, silently giving him the opportunity to air his gripe. Thankfully, his friend remained quiet.

Not that Mal didn't understand what Raine was going through. He did. Hell, before he found Callie, Raine had suffered as much as Mal. And he'd fed his grief by taking risks over and over and over again. He'd died more times than Mal could count, and each time he was reborn in the phoenix fire with a new tattoo to mark the birth.

Now there was hardly any skin on Raine that wasn't inked, and each tat evidenced death, rebirth—and how damn close Raine now was to losing his humanity.

Because while the brotherhood's bodies were immortal, that didn't mean there wasn't a price. Burn too many times, and the phoenix fire would burn out their humanity as well. It had happened only once before— to a brother named Samson who now lived a mindless, violent existence in the brotherhood's facility in Germany.

It didn't happen slowly, with each death taking a brother that much closer to the void of madness. On the contrary, it happened all at once, and the only warning was a sensation of spreading darkness during a burn that signaled the coming end.

Samson had described the feeling before falling into madness on his very next burn.

And Mal knew that Raine was close as well.

Jessica scowled at Raine. "Don't you dare be upset with Mal for not sending you. What if the fuerie do come? What if you have to fight? Are you really such an asshole that you'd risk Callie losing you so soon after you two have found each other again?"

Raine sunk down a bit into his seat. "She's worth every sacrifice," he said. "But that doesn't mean that I don't miss kicking ass."

"And that you're pissed because I sent Dante instead of you," Mal added, hoping to lighten the mood.

Raine snorted. "True that."

"Raine or Dante, it's all the same," Asher said, his words slow and easy as he finally joined the conversation. "Mal shouldn't have sent anyone."

"You know damn well the fuerie will swoop her up in a heartbeat given the opportunity. I couldn't let her go alone."

"You shouldn't have let her go at all." Ash pushed his chair back from the table and stood. "You should have taken your blade to her, Mal. You know damn well what she is."

"She's my mate." Mal stood, too, fury rising within him.

"You're thinking with your cock." Asher looked from Mal to the rest of the group. "And you're all letting him."

Mal forced himself to stay still—to not leap across the table and throttle his friend, because dammit, that's exactly what he wanted to do.

"Goddammit," Ash said. "You all know what can happen. Don't you remember Chani?"

Some of the tension left Mal—of course Ash would be thinking of Chani. He'd grown so close to the Egyptian servant girl who had tended him after the fuerie had captured and tortured him.

But Chani had been killed in 365 when Mal had been too slow, and Christina had lost control and caused the earthquake that had leveled the Port of Alexandria.

"She's different this time," Liam said gently. "Mal and I made the decision as to how to handle it together. You know that, Ash. I briefed you."

"You did," Ash agreed. "Doesn't mean you made the right decision."

"I understand where you're coming from," Mal said. "And I sympathize. But that's not your call to make."

For a moment, Ash was silent. Then he inclined his head, just slightly. "No, it's not my call." He lifted his face to meet Mal's eyes. "But maybe it should be."

CHAPTER 10

I'VE BEEN AWAKE for at least half an hour, but I'm still in bed snuggled down among the fluffy pillows and crisp sheets, warm inside this cocoon of sensuality.

I sigh, then stretch, then try to think of a reason why I should get out of bed when I still have at least two hours before I have to leave for rehearsal.

Honestly, nothing is coming to mind. It's too nice here, and I am still savoring last night's delicious dream.

The truth is that I've had more erotic dreams since I moved in with Brayden than I have in my entire life. The one last night, however, was the first in which I knew the identity of the gray-eyed man.

Malcolm.

I close my eyes and sigh, letting my hand slide down between my thighs, remembering the way the Malcolm in my dream had touched me there, stroking and kissing and then, thank god, finally thrusting so hard and deep inside me that I actually came awake from the force of the orgasm that ripped through me in my sleep.

I sigh again, giving in to pure pleasure.

But now that I'm no longer living in the world of dreams, my satisfaction is tainted. I may not understand *what* is between Mal and me, but I have no doubt that something is going on there. A connection. An attraction.

Maybe it's just lust and hormones, but maybe it's more.

And Mal made it perfectly clear last night that as far as he's concerned it's real and it's solid and he doesn't intend to let it go.

I remember the intensity with which he looked into my eyes. The longing and the heat. The passion and the desire.

But there was more, too. There was affection and humor.

Hell, there might even have been love. Which is ridiculous because he barely knows me.

Or maybe he knows you better than you think. Better than you want to believe.

Frustrated with myself, I swing my feet out of the bed, both because I really should get up, and because I am hoping that physical motion might just push the random thoughts from my head. Because the truth is that Malcolm is the kind of man for whom I just might break my own rules. But letting go and getting close and trusting him to protect my heart is a hard journey for me, and I can't think about it too much or else I'll just end up scaring myself right out of the possibility.

I want him, it's as simple as that. And as complicated. Because what if I agree to try and make it work between us, but then I end up closing myself off? We'll lose this magical, joyous connection between us.

But how can I just keep him as a friend when it's clear we both want so much more?

I hear rattling from the kitchen and the sound is like an invitation to spill my problems to Brayden. And not just my problems, but to finally tell him the truth about me and relationships. I'll lay it all out for him, and then I'll let Doctor Kline diagnose my love life and help me decide on the right treatment.

And if that doesn't work, at least I'll have had my fair share of the bacon.

I head toward the kitchen in bare feet wearing only my sleep shirt. I can already smell the bacon, so I expect to find Brayden at the stove making either pancakes or scrambled eggs.

Instead, I find Malcolm—and my breath catches in my throat.

He hasn't yet noticed me yet, and I stand there, soaking up the sight of him. He's casual in only jeans and a T-shirt, and I can't help but appreciate the way his ass fills out those jeans and the way his shoulders complete the line of the shirt.

He moves with an efficient grace, and I lean against the wall and soak it all in, enjoying the way this feels. The two of us. A kitchen. Breakfast. It feels warm and nice and real, and I hug myself tight, as if it's necessary to hold in this swell of happiness that is building inside me.

Then Mal breaks the spell with a heartfelt, "Well, fuck," and I turn my attention to the counter where he has mangled an omelette in the process of plating it.

"I'm sure it still tastes good," I say, trying not to laugh.

He turns to me, and despite the fact that he is obviously irritated by eggs and pans and plates and stoves, I see only pleasure in his face. "Good morning."

"Good morning to you, too. Where's Brayden?"

"I traded privacy with you for Dagny's phone number," Mal says. "Worked like a charm."

I laugh. "I bet it did," I say, then nod toward the plate. "Is that for me?"

"I'd thought I might bring it to you in bed," he says. "But I think we'll be lucky if I manage to get something edible on the table."

I laugh, then sit at the place he makes for me. "Are you having some?"

"I had a bagel on my way over. But I thought you deserved a nice breakfast. You'd think after so many years, I'd be better at this…"

He trails off with a shrug. "Anyway, hopefully it tastes better than it looks."

It does, actually. It's cheesy and cooked just enough, and when I tell him it's perfect, I can't help but melt a little at the look of soft appreciation on his face. I take another bite, and then stand up and go to where he's leaning casually against the kitchen counter.

"Done?"

"Not even close," I say. Because right then, it's not breakfast that I want. I want to finish last night. I want to fulfill my dream.

Maybe I'll regret it, I don't know. But I'm more certain that I'll regret not having him. Right here. Right now.

"No?" I see amusement—and understanding—in his eyes.

"Listen," I say. "About last night. I kind of bolted on you, and—" I clear my throat. "This time I won't bolt."

"Is that a fact?"

I nod. And I'm about to say something when he speaks first, his words shocking me to silence. "Take off your nightshirt."

"What?" I look at him, leaning against the stone countertop, his hands tucked into his pockets and his eyes full of heat and power and promise.

"You heard me." The corner of his mouth quirks up. "Or you could just bolt."

I narrow my eyes, because now he's thrown down a gauntlet and I have no choice. "All right," I say. And then, before I can talk myself out of it, I take the hem of my sleep shirt and pull it up and over my head. I do it fast, like tugging off a bandage, and then let it drop to the floor.

I'm naked now—no socks, no under-wear, no bra. And though my instinct is to cross my arms over my chest, I don't. And my bravery is immediately rewarded by the look of pure adoration that I see on his face.

"Christina… lover, you are exquisite."

His words wash over me, making me shiver.

"Cold?" he asks.

I start to say no, then realize that would be idiotic. Instead, I say, "Warm me?"

It is an invitation he doesn't hesitate to accept, and he moves quickly to me, then gathers me in his arms. "Dear god, how I've wanted to feel you again. To touch you again."

"It was just last night," I say with a laugh.

"Was it?" He tilts his head to meet my eyes. "To me, it feels like forever."

"Oh." The word is as tremulous as I feel. As if the simplest touch or the sweetest kiss could send me over the edge.

And when he does kiss me, there is no denying that I've missed this, too. Maybe it was only last night, but I am hungry for him. Starved.

"Please," I beg. "Touch me."

"Where?" I hear the tease in his voice.

"Everywhere."

He grabs me by the waist and lifts me to the counter, then gently spreads my legs.

"Mal." There is a tremor in my voice, and I gasp when a wave of pure pleasure crashes over me as he brushes his lips up my inner thigh, then kisses me intimately, his tongue teasing my clit so that I squirm, wanting more than just this soft tease. And when he thrusts his tongue deep inside me, I feel the pressure of passion building inside me.

"More," I beg. "Please. I don't care if it's fast—we can go slow later. I just want you. Wild and hard and now."

"Anything you want," he says, rising up and kissing me as my fingers find the button of his jeans and slowly ease his zipper down.

I ease his cock free, holding and stroking its long, hard length. That velvet steel that I crave, so much so that my sex is throbbing in anticipation.

"Do you have a condom?" My words are barely breath.

For a minute, I think he looks surprised, then his expression clears and he reaches into the back pocket of his jeans and extracts a foil-wrapped condom. Which, I'm happy to see, looks like it's been tucked in there for quite a long time.

He sheaths himself, and I can stand it no longer. "Now," I beg, shifting on the counter to get close to him, then sighing in pleasure as he clasps his hands on my hips and roughly scoots me to the edge. He thrusts inside me and I arch back with the movement, taking him in, wanting all of him. Wanting him as deep as he can go.

I hook my legs around him, and he groans as the motion forces him even deeper inside me.

"I can't hold back. I have no strength to

hold out for you. I want you too damn bad."

"Then don't," I say. "Please. I want to feel it. I want to feel you explode."

He pounds into me, each motion finding that sweet spot in my core, sending me spiraling higher. Until it is not just him who will explode, but me as well. Because I swear I am going to come with more force and passion than I have ever experienced before.

There is power and wildness, electricity and pyrotechnics building inside me. A wild force. A goddamn electrical storm. And it's spinning and spinning, higher and higher. And my entire body is heating and—

"Mal! Oh, god, Mal!"

Even as the orgasm takes me, I feel the weight of it drain from me, the heat, the sparks, everything dissipating, as if a balloon has popped inside me.

It was like nothing I've ever experienced before, but I can't deny that I like it, especially this wild, drained, exhaustion that makes me feel like I was well and truly fucked.

"Wow," I say. "I'm glad we did it fast. I'm not sure I could have survived much longer with you."

"I promise you'll survive just fine."

He gathers me up, and as he does, I feel a burst of static electricity that makes my entire body tingle and my hairs stand on end. It's an odd but not unpleasant sensation, and I snuggle against his chest, feeling warm and happy. And, strangely, I feel protected, too.

Once we are settled on the couch, I look up at him again and see my own pleasure matched in his eyes. Pleasure, yes, but something else, too.

"Is something wrong?"

"Not a thing," he says as he pulls me close and spreads Brayden's quilt over us.

"Mmm." I burrow against him. "This is wonderful, but I need to get dressed and get to rehearsal."

"Stay with me."

I laugh. "No can do, and you shouldn't want me to, Mr. Investor." I shift so that

I'm on top of him. "But I promise to come back."

"Juliet. Star-crossed lovers. It's never been one of my favorites."

I raise my brows. "No?"

He meets my eyes. "I don't like unhappy endings."

I brush a kiss over his lips. "I'm very glad to hear you say that. But right now, I really do have to go."

I climb off him, but he takes my hand and tugs me back.

"Mal!" There's laughter in my voice, but it dies when I see the expression on his face. "Something is wrong."

"You can go to rehearsal, but I'm going to go with you."

I frown, but I don't argue. "Um, okay."

"And when I say that I want you to stay with me, I mean that I want you to move in with me. That's the easiest way to keep you safe."

He's sitting up now, and I move to sit next to him. "What the hell are you talking about?"

"You asked me last night what I do—the truth is, that I run a security company. Phoenix Security. Personal protection is high on our list of services. And we've been charged with keeping you safe."

"Safe?" I scoot over to the far corner of the couch. "What are you talking about?"

"There are people who believe you have something they want. And they will kill you to retrieve it."

"I don't know what you're talking about."

"I believe you," he says. "The people who are after you don't."

"What people?"

"An organization. They call themselves the fuerie."

"Fury?" I stand up, holding tight to the blanket to cover me, because right now I don't want to be naked. "That's crazy."

"It's the truth."

"They'll kill me? Your story doesn't make sense. If they kill me, how would they get this MacGuffin?"

"Christina, you have to believe me. I want to protect you from them—from everything. And you will be safest if you're at my side." His voice is so irritatingly calm and even that I want to scream. More than that, I want to cry. Because a moment that was perfect only seconds ago has now gone completely off the rails.

"Dammit, Mal, do you have any idea how whacked this sounds?" I do. My mother saw conspiracies around every corner. And I'm sure she believed there were people who wanted me dead. The devil was inside me after all. "And come on, you're guarding me? What are you, a charitable security company? Because I didn't hire you. So who did?"

"That's actually confidential. But I assure you it's legitimate. Though not everyone at the company agrees that we should have taken your case."

"Oh, of course not." I try another tact. "I just left last night. You didn't follow me. I grabbed a taxi and came home all by myself."

"I had you tailed."

"You *what?*"

He nods to the window. "I promise, you've been looked after."

I head to the window.

"He's gone," Mal says. "I'm here."

I draw in a breath, trying to decide what to do. Trying not to completely freak out.

"Look," he says, his voice so reasonable I want to slap him. "Maybe I shouldn't have told you. But you have a right to know. Either way, I want you to move in with me."

"We barely know each other."

"We know each other a lot more than barely."

I frown. I'd thought we did. Now I wasn't so sure.

"Check out the company," he says, pulling a business card out of his wallet. "Go get dressed. Log onto a computer and check us out. Hell, Google us. We're reputable. We're the best. For that matter, Google me." He pauses, and he looks so earnest that for a moment I believe his completely freakish tale. "I'll take you to rehearsal, we can talk after, and we'll go from there. Okay?"

I nod. I have absolutely no idea what I'm going to do, but I do know that my world is shattering around me. Funny that it takes finding out that the guy I'm attracted to might be a complete psycho in order to figure out the extent of my feelings for him.

But I can't think about that now. I need to just think about what to do next.

And although I know very little right now, one thing that I am certain of is that standing in the living room wearing nothing but a blanket isn't part of my next move.

CHAPTER 11

I PACE THE length of my bedroom, trying to decide what to do.

Last night it was shared energy and past lives, and now assassins? That's insane—I mean, I know crazy, and right now I'm staring it in the face.

My heart twists and I force myself not to cry. Because dammit, this was a man I think I could have crossed my line for. I could have dated him. Fallen for him.

I could have given him my heart and trusted him not to break it.

But if I almost gave my trust to a man who is just as fucked up as my mother was, then what the hell does that make me?

As crazy as she was.

Fuck.

I need to move. Need to just get out of here.

Hell, I need to run.

Maybe not forever—I'm not that much of a coward. But I need time to think. To figure out what I'm going to do.

To figure out how I can push him away. How I can end this thing between us even before it has really started.

And—oh, god—I have to figure out how I can continue being Juliet when the very Romeo I'm running from is one of the owners of the goddamn theater.

Not only crazy, but a stalker, too.

Christ, I am so fucked.

Except I don't want to believe it.

Hell, I *don't* believe it. Not any of it. Not that some bad guys are after me. Not that Malcolm is crazy. Not that he's stalking me or would want to hurt me or that he would ever do anything other than protect me.

I know him.

I hitch in a breath as a tear trickles down my cheek.

Dammit, I *know* him. And, yes, despite everything, I trust him.

The problem is that I don't know myself. Do I trust him because I see the true core of him and know that he would never cause me harm? Or do I trust him because I'm deluded and have, like my mother before me, constructed a fantasy world in which I now live. And which will, if I'm not careful, end up killing me.

I don't know. Right now, I feel like I don't know anything.

And so I give in to the urge to run and hope that as my feet pound the pavement and my lungs draw in the air, that maybe somehow I'll find an answer, if not inside myself, then out there in the world.

MAL SIPPED A cup of coffee while he waited, trying to keep his nerves steady.

The stakes were rising—and while he'd loved the sensation of feeling her come in his arms, the underlying current of energy pulsing through the weapon had put a definite strain on the encounter. And forced him to show part of his hand before he wanted to.

But whatever it took to get her to move in with him. Because the weapon was too close to the surface right now. And if he wanted to justify keeping her alive, he had to make sure that he kept the energy at bay.

Thank goodness he'd been right about having more control. He'd been able to draw out her energy. To dampen the effect so that the weapon settled even as she did.

She'd been more limp and sated than she was probably used to after sex, but with luck she'd simply write that off to his skill as a lover.

He half-smiled. How was that for making lemonade out of lemons?

But in truth, the situation wasn't without its possibilities. And while keeping the weapon tamped down had to be his priority, he already knew that the way to do that was to teach her control. To keep her on the edge, teasing her, but not letting her come. Not until she could control it so specifically that she came on his command—a command he would give only when he was ready to draw the energy from her and keep the weapon safe.

He took another sip as he considered, feeling himself grow hard at the erotic possibilities. Hell, he could imagine her, bound to his bed, a willing pupil to his tutelage.

Then again, they could simply not have sex at all. But that was an unacceptable approach for several reasons, not the least of which being that he didn't think it would work. Now that he was with her—now that they were both so hyperaware of each other—basic, pure, primal desire would take over. They could try abstinence, but he doubted it would work. And if she was sexually frustrated and did anything to relieve that stress when he wasn't around—

He shuddered.

No. He fully intended to be with her 24/7 until the weapon was dealt with.

And if they needed to work off some sexual tension to make sure she didn't go nuclear unexpectedly, then he would enthusiastically rise to the task.

Hell, they'd had so little time to explore these bodies before she was taken from him so many millennia ago. Now, not only did they have the time to explore, but they needed to. Because her passion was tied to the weapon, and teaching her control and submission would be not only a pleasure but a necessity.

Control.

He pictured Christina beneath him, submitting to his will, learning to control her own pleasure until he gave her permission for release.

Trusting him.

They both needed that, he thought. After so many years of fear and heartbreak, they both needed to know that she trusted him completely. And she needed to know that he would always take care of her.

They could do this. Together, they would make this plan work.

No more rising energy. No more pulsing danger.

No more fear that it would be Alexandria all over again, and—

Oh, shit.

The weapon's energy had risen. Yes, he'd tamped it down. Yes, he'd stopped it.

But there had been a danger.

And Asher would surely have felt it.

And, dammit, so would the fuerie.

Fuck.

Even now, Ash was probably cornering Liam and pleading his case that Christina had to be destroyed.

He glanced at his watch, then frowned. "Christina," he called out. "We need to make a stop before rehearsal. Come on. We need to go." He kept his voice calm, but he wanted to get out of there. If the fuerie were coming, he wanted to be in his own house, with its protections and weapons. Not ten floors up in an unfamiliar building.

He waited for her response, his frown deepening when none came.

"Christina?"

Fuck.

He started down the hallway when his phone beeped, signaling a text.

It was from Dante. And all it said was *911.*

Their signal—and it meant he'd sensed the presence of fuerie.

Without knocking, Mal pushed open the door to her bedroom.

"Christina!" he shouted. But it didn't matter.

There were fuerie coming—and she'd gone out alone.

I BURST OUT of the service entrance at a dead run.

The truth is I don't know where I'm going—especially since it's myself I truly want to run from.

But the sensation of moving seems to help. I only want to get away. To escape.

And as I race around the building toward the street, I think that maybe I should just go to a movie. Find a dark theater and sit in it and eat popcorn all day.

Not a bad idea, actually, and I'm trying to remember where the closest theater is when I turn the corner and stop short. Because right in front of me is a very round little man. And he has a face that seems made of fire.

I skid to a stop, then turn back the way I came. There's something familiar about this moment, as if I'd seen him before. But I don't stop to ponder that feeling because when you see someone with a face of flame, you don't think—you run. And now that I'm heading the opposite direction, I'm picking up speed.

Not enough, though, because I feel the

flame man's hand close around my upper arm and yank me backwards.

I stumble, then fall on my ass even as someone unseen grabs the flame man and tugs him into the shadows.

"Mal!" I scream his name, only realizing as the name passes my lips that my savior isn't Mal at all.

But I know this man, this savior.

The copper hair. The piercing eyes.

Asher.

"Thank you," I say. "Oh, god, thank you."

But he is paying no attention to me. Instead, he takes what looks like a switch-blade from his pocket. Only when he extends the knife, I see that it's not a short blade at all. Instead, it's the length of a sword and seems to be made of forged light.

And as I remain sprawled on the ground, he takes his sword or lightsaber or whatever it is and stabs it through the heart of the fallen flame man—who immediately combusts, leaving nothing to mark the moment other than a small pile of gray dust.

Apparently the jury is in—I really have gone completely insane.

I scramble to my feet, wanting nothing more in that moment than to get inside—to get to Mal.

"If you get them through the heart, they disintegrate," Asher says conversationally. "Anywhere else, and you have to deal with a body."

I gape at him, not at all certain what I should say to that. "Um."

I clear my throat and try again. "I—Mal's upstairs. I—we should go. We need to tell him." I need to hear from him that this is real and I'm not crazy.

"Wait," Asher says.

I hesitate. My gut is telling me to run, but Asher just saved me from the flame man, so I figure I owe him at least some basic courtesy.

"Did Mal tell you?" he asks. "Who that guy was, I mean. Did he tell you who was after you? Did he tell you why?"

I lick my lips. I'm starting to get the feeling that I'm not crazy. Which is good.

But I'm also afraid that I'm in the middle of something very, very strange.

And that part is bad.

"Christina?" Asher presses. "Did he tell you?"

I shove my hands into the pockets of the jeans I'd put on. "Just that his security company is trying to protect me. That some group is trying to kidnap me. But he hasn't said why. He said it's too long a story."

"No," Ash says. "It's not long at all. They want you because you're a weapon."

I don't have time to ask what the fuck he's talking about before he continues.

"It's too dangerous to keep you around, Christina. Mal's fucked this one up, and leader or not, I can't let him risk the world. And I'm sorry, because I know you don't remember it, but you and I used to be pretty good friends. But you'll come back. Mal will see you again. And the odds are damn good that you won't remember any of this."

I shake my head, because I don't have a clue what he's talking about.

At the same time, though, I take a step backward. Because while I don't understand what he means, I'm pretty damn sure that it doesn't end in warm fuzzes for me.

I only get one step when he extends that freakish sword again.

I burst forward, drawing on all my strength, but I'd seen how fast he moved with the flame man, and I know that there's no way I'll get away from him.

A wave of terror crests over me, so potent I can taste it like bile on my tongue. The fear is hot and boiling. Like it's not only going to fill me, but it's going to explode out of me, wild and red and utterly dangerous.

The weapon.

Oh, dear god, he was right. It's not fear that I'm feeling, not entirely. It's the weapon, too. And I have no idea how to control it, and—

I scream as I see a sword arcing through the air toward me. And for just a split second, I think that maybe it's a good thing, because if the weapon inside me gets out—and it will, because I don't know how to control it, and—

—And then Asher's sword falls to the ground even as his mouth hangs open in surprise.

I watch, confused, as he topples to the ground, and the next thing I see through the building red haze is Mal rushing toward me, shouting for me to back it down, back it down!

I can't. I don't know how!

But then he's holding me, and the redness is fading, the wildness sliding back inside.

It's Mal—somehow, he's doing this. He's holding me. Touching me.

He's saving me.

I feel a tear trickle down my cheek, then taste salt when Mal presses his lips to mine in a gentle kiss.

When he pulls away, I nod toward the circle of fire that is consuming Ash's body.

I'm not scared or bewildered. I know that it is phoenix fire. That it will destroy and regenerate.

That Asher will be back.

I tilt my head to look up at Mal through a veil of tears. "You didn't kill me this time."

I see the surprise on his face. "You remember?"

And with a shock, I realize that, yes, I do. "Some of it, at least. It's strange." I frown as I try to explain. "It's like remembering a movie that you mostly slept through. I've got bits and pieces, but not the whole thread. And it doesn't feel like the memory belongs to me. I know the memories are mine, but I'm Jaynie, too. And everyone else I've been born as over the years." I frown. "It's a lot of memories. I don't know if I can keep them all." I clutch his hand. "What if I lose them? What if I forget?"

"You might," he says, drawing me close and wrapping his arms around me. "You have before. But it doesn't matter. I love all of you. Christina, Jaynie, and everyone in between. And I will always keep you safe. *We* will keep you safe."

I actually laugh as he pulls me close, and I let his words soak in. *Love.*

He said he loves me. The word makes me smile—and, yes, it terrifies me a little, too.

It's a big step, after all, and one I'm not sure I'm ready for. Certainly, I'm not ready to say it. But with Mal, I know I want to try and get there.

I suck in a breath, my eyes still drawn to that circle of fire. "Maybe you should have let him do it." I squeeze his hand. "I don't want to be the woman who ends the world."

"You won't be. I promise that we can control this."

"How?"

"Do you trust me?"

And for the first time in my life, I don't hesitate to say it. "Yes. I trust you." What I don't say is that I might just love him, too.

But there is time enough for that. With Mal, there is always enough time.

I hope you enjoyed the first part of Mal and Christina's story. I'd be thrilled if you'd leave a review at your favorite retailer!

And be sure to find out what happens next for these star-crossed lovers in the next two novellas in the trilogy:

Find Me in Pleasure

Find Me in Passion

And if you missed Callie and Raine's story, Caress of Darkness, be sure to grab a copy now!

Finally, don't close this book yet! Keep reading for the first chapter of Caress of Darkness plus a special bonus: An excerpt from Tattered Loyalties *by New York Times bestselling author Carrie Ann Ryan that you're sure to enjoy!*

Please enjoy this first chapter from Raine and Callie's story:

CARESS OF DARKNESS

A Dark Pleasures novella

By

Julie Kenner

CHAPTER 1

"WHO THE FUCK are you?"

I jump, startled by the voice—deep and male and undeniably irritated—that echoes across the forest of boxes scattered throughout my father's SoHo antique store.

"Who am I?" I repeat as I stand and search the shadows for the intruder. "Who the hell are you?"

There is more bravado in my voice than I feel, especially when I finally see the man who has spoken. He is standing in the shadows near the front door—a door that I am damn sure I locked after putting the Closed sign in the window and settling in for a long night of inventory and packing.

He is tall, well over six feet, with a lean, muscular build that is accentuated by the faded jeans that hug his thighs and the simple white T-shirt that reveals muscled arms sleeved with tattoos.

His casual clothes, inked skin, and close-shaved head hint at danger and rebellion, but those traits are contrasted by a commanding, almost elegant, presence that seems to both fill the room and take charge of it. This is a man who would be equally at ease in a tux as a T-shirt. A man who expects the world to bend to his will, and if it doesn't comply, he will go out and bend it himself.

I see that confidence most potently in his face, all sharp lines and angles that blend together into a masterpiece now dusted with the shadow of a late afternoon beard. He has the kind of eyes that miss nothing, and right now they are hard and assessing. They are softened, however, by the kind of long, dark lashes that most women would kill for.

His mouth is little more than a hard slash across his features, but I see a hint of softness, and when I find myself wondering how those lips would feel against my skin, I realize that I have been staring and yank myself firmly from my reverie.

"I asked you a question," I snap, more harshly than I intended. "Who are you, and how did you get in here?"

"Raine," he says, striding toward me. "Rainer Engel. And I walked in through the front door."

"I locked it." I wipe my now-sweaty hands on my dusty yoga pants.

"The fact that I'm inside suggests otherwise."

He has crossed the store in long, efficient strides, and now stands in front of me. I catch his scent, all musk and male, sin and sensuality, and feel an unwelcome ache between my thighs.

Not unwelcome because I don't like sex. On the contrary, I'd have to label myself a fan, and an overenthusiastic one at that.

Because the truth is that I've spent too many nights in the arms of too many strangers trying to fill some void in myself.

I say "some void" because I don't really know what I'm searching for. A connection, I guess, but at the same time I'm scared of finding one and ending up hurt, which is why I shy from traditional "my friend has a friend" kind of dating, and spend more time than I should in bars and clubs. And that means that while I might be enjoying a series of really good lays, I'm not doing anything more than using sex as a Band-Aid.

At least, that is what my therapist, Kelly, back home in Austin says. And since I'm a lawyer and not a shrink, I'm going to have to take her word on that.

"We're closed," I say firmly. Or, rather, I intend to say firmly. In fact, my voice comes out thin, suggesting a question rather than a command.

Not that my tone matters. The man—*Raine*—seems entirely uninterested in what I have to say.

He cocks his head slightly to one side, as if taking my measure, and if the small curve of that sensual mouth is any indication, he likes what he sees. I prop a hand on my hip and stare back defiantly. I know what I look like—and I know that with a few exceptions, men tend to go stupid when I dial it up.

The ratty law school T-shirt I'm wearing is tight, accenting breasts that I'd cursed in high school, but that had become a boon once I started college and realized that my ample tits, slender waist, and long legs added up to a combination that made guys drool. Add in wavy blonde hair and green eyes and I've got the kind of cheerleader-esque good looks that make so many of the good old boy lawyers in Texas think that I've got cotton candy for brains.

And believe me when I say that I'm not shy about turning their misogynistic stereotype to my advantage, both in the courtroom and out of it.

"You're Callie." His voice conveys absolute certainty, as if his inspection confirmed one of the basic facts of the universe. Which, since I *am* Callie, I guess it did. But how the hell he knows who I am is beyond me.

"Your father talks about you a lot," Raine says, apparently picking up on my confusion. His eyes rake over me as he speaks, and my skin prickles with awareness, as potent as if his fingertip had stroked me. "A lawyer who lives in Texas with the kind of looks that make a father nervous, balanced by sharp, intelligent eyes that reassure him that she's not going to do anything stupid."

"You know my father."

"I know your father," he confirms.

"And he told you that about me?"

"The lawyer part. The rest I figured out all on my own." One corner of his mouth curves up. "I have eyes, after all." Those eyes are currently aimed at my chest, and I say a silent thank you to whoever decided that padded bras were a good thing because otherwise he would certainly see how hard and tight my nipples have become.

"University of Texas School of Law. Good school." He lifts his gaze from my chest to my face, and the heat I see in those ice blue eyes seems to seep under my skin, melting me a bit from the inside out. "Very good."

I lick my lips, realizing that my mouth has gone uncomfortably dry. I've been working as an assistant district attorney for the last two years. I've gotten used to being the one in charge of a room. And right now, I'm feeling decidedly off-kilter, part of me wanting to pull him close, and the other wanting to run as far and as fast from him as I can.

Since neither option is reasonable at the moment, I simply take a step back, then find myself trapped by the glass jewelry case, now pressing against my ass.

I clear my throat. "Listen, Mr. Engel, if you're looking for my father—"

"I am, and I apologize for snapping at you when I came in, but I was surprised to see that the shop was closed, and when I saw someone other than Oliver moving inside, I got worried."

"I closed early so that I could work without being interrupted."

A hint of a smile plays at his mouth. "In that case, I'll also apologize for interrupting. But Oliver asked me to come by when I got back in town. I'm anxious to discuss the amulet that he's located."

"Oh." I don't know why I'm surprised. He obviously hadn't come into the store looking for me. And yet for some reason the fact that I've suddenly become irrelevant rubs me the wrong way.

Clearly, I need to get a grip, and I paste on my best customer service smile. "I'm really sorry, but my dad's not here."

"No? I told him I'd come straight over." I can hear the irritation in his voice. "He knows how much I want this piece—how much I'm willing to pay. If he's made arrangements to sell it to another—"

"*No.*" The word is fast and firm and

entirely unexpected. "It's not like that. My dad doesn't play games with clients."

"That's true. He doesn't." His brow creases as he looks around the shop, taking in the open boxes, half filled with inventory, the colored sticky notes I've been using to informally assign items to numbered boxes, and the general disarray of the space. "Callie. What's happened to your father?"

It is the way he says my name that loosens my tongue. Had he simply asked the question, I probably would have told him that he could come back in the morning and we'd search the computerized inventory for the piece he's looking for. But there is something so intimate about my name on his lips that I can't help but answer honestly.

"My dad had a stroke last week." My voice hitches as I speak, and I look off toward the side of the store, too wrecked to meet his eyes directly.

"Oh, Callie." He steps closer and takes my hand, and I'm surprised to find that I not only don't pull away, but that I actually have to fight the urge to pull our joint hands close to my heart.

"I didn't know," he says. "I'm so sorry. How is he doing?"

"N-not very well." I suck in a breath and try to gather myself, but it's just so damn hard. My mom walked out when I was four, saying that being a mother was too much responsibility, and ever since I've been my dad's entire world. It's always amazed me that he didn't despise me. But he really doesn't. He says that I was a gift, and I know it's true because I have seen and felt it every day of my life.

Whatever the cause of my disconnect with men, it doesn't harken back to my dad, a little fact that I know fascinates my shrink, though she's too much the professional to flat out tell me as much.

"Does he have decent care? Do you need any referrals? Any help financially?" Raine is crouching in front of me, and I realize that I have sunk down, so that my butt is on the cold tile floor and I am hugging my knees.

I shake my head, a bit dazed to realize this stranger is apparently offering to help pay my dad's medical bills. "We're fine. He's got great care and great insurance. He's just—" I break off as my voice cracks. "*Shit.*"

"Hey, it's okay. Breathe now. That's it, just breathe." He presses his hands to my shoulders, and his face is just inches away. His eyes are wide and safe and warm, and I want to slide into them. To just disappear into a place where there are neither worries nor responsibilities. Where someone strong will hold me and take care of me and make everything bad disappear.

But that's impossible, and so I draw another breath in time with his words and try once again to formulate a coherent thought. "He's—he's got good doctors, really. But he's not lucid. And this is my dad. I mean, Oliver Sinclair hasn't gone a day in his life without an opinion or a witticism."

I feel the tears well in my eyes and I

swipe them away with a brusque brush of my thumb. "And it kills me because I can look at him and it breaks my heart to know that he must have all this stuff going on inside his head that he just can't say, and—and—"

But I can't get the words out, and I feel the tears snaking down my cheeks, and dammit, dammit, *dammit*, I do not want to lose it in front of this man—this stranger who doesn't feel like a stranger.

His grip on my shoulders tightens and he leans toward me.

And then—oh, dear god—his lips are on mine and they are as warm and soft as I'd imagined and he's kissing me so gently and so sweetly that all my worries are just melting away and I'm limp in his arms.

"Shhh. It's okay." His voice washes over me, as gentle and calming as a summer rain. "Everything's going to be okay."

I breathe deep, soothed by the warm sensuality of this stranger's golden voice. Except he isn't a stranger. I may not have met him before today, but somehow, here in his arms, I *know* him.

And that, more than anything, comforts me.

Calmer, I tilt my head back and meet his eyes. It is a soft moment and a little sweet— but it doesn't stay that way. It changes in the space of a glance. In the instant of a heartbeat. And what started out as gentle comfort transforms into fiery heat.

I don't know which of us moves first. All I know is that I have to claim him and be claimed by him. That I have to taste him— consume him. Because in some essential way that I don't fully understand, I know that only this man can quell the need burning inside me, and I lose myself in the hot intensity of his mouth upon mine. Of his tongue demanding entrance, and his lips, hard and demanding, forcing me to give everything he wants to take.

I am limp against him, felled by the onslaught of erotic sparks that his kisses have scattered through me. I am lost in the sensation of his hands stroking my back. Of his chest pressed against my breasts.

But it isn't until I realize that he has pulled me into his lap and that I can feel the hard demand of his erection against my rear that I force myself to escape this sensual reality and scramble backward out of his embrace.

"I'm sorry," I say, my breath coming too hard.

"Callie—" The need I hear in his voice reflects my own, and I clench my hands into fists as I fight against the instinct to move back into his arms.

"No." I don't understand what's happening—this instant heat, like a match striking gasoline. I've never reacted to a man this way before. My skin feels prickly, as if I've been caught in a lightning storm. His scent is all over me. And the taste of him lingers on my mouth.

And oh, dear god, I'm wet, my body literally aching with need, with a primal desire for him to just rip my clothes off and take me right there on the hard, dusty floor.

He's triggered a wildness in me that I don't understand—and my reaction scares the hell out of me.

"You need to go," I say, and I am astonished that my words are both measured and articulate, as if I'm simply announcing that it is closing time to a customer.

He stays silent, but I shake my head anyway, and hold up a finger as if in emphasis.

"No," I say, in response to nothing. "I don't know anything about this amulet. And now you really need to leave. Please," I add. "Please, Raine. I need you to go."

For a moment he only looks at me. Then he nods, a single tilt of his head in acknowledgment. "All right," he says very softly. "I'll go. But I'm not ever leaving you again."

I stand frozen, as if his inexplicable words have locked me in place. He turns slowly and strides out of the shop without looking back. And when the door clicks into place behind him and I am once again alone, I gulp in air as tears well in my eyes again.

I rub my hands over my face, forgiving myself for this emotional miasma because of all the shit that's happened with my dad. Of course I'm a wreck; what daughter wouldn't be?

Determined to get a grip, I follow his path to the door, then hold onto the knob. I'd come over intending to lock it. But now I have to fight the urge to yank it open and beg him to return.

It's an urge I fight. It's just my grief talking. My fear that I'm about to lose my father, the one person in all the world who is close to me, and so I have clung to a stranger in a desperate effort to hold fast to something.

That, at least, is what my shrink would say. *You're fabricating a connection in order to fill a void. It's what you do, Callie. It's what you've always done when lonely and afraid.*

I nod, telling myself I agree with Kelly's voice in my head.

And I do.

Because I am lonely.

And I am afraid of losing my dad.

But that's not the whole of it. Because there's something else that I'm afraid of, too, though I cannot put my finger on it. A strange sense of something coming. Something dark. Something bad.

And what scares me most is the ridiculous, unreasonable fear that I have just pushed away the one person I need to survive whatever is waiting for me out there in the dark.

Want to read more?
Visit the Dark Pleasures page on Julie's website.
http://juliekenner.com/jks-books/dark-pleasures/

JK'S BOOKLIST

I hope you enjoyed *Find Me in Darkness*! If you think your friends or other readers would enjoy the book, I'd be honored if you'd rate or "like" the book or leave a review at your favorite retailers. And, of course, I'm always thrilled if you want to spread the word through Twitter, Facebook or other social media outlets.

Questions about the book, or me, or the meaning of the universe? I'd love to hear from you. You can reach me via email at juliekenner@gmail.com or on Twitter (I'm @juliekenner) or through Facebook at www.facebook.com/JulieKennerBooks or www.facebook.com/JKennerBooks

Don't want to miss any of my books or news? Be sure to sign up for my newsletter. You can use this link to the newsletter (http://eepurl.com/-tfoP) or go to my website, www.juliekenner.com

I've written a lot of books, and most of them are available in digital format. Here's a list of just a few (you can find more at my website!); I hope you check them out!

Kate Connor Demon-Hunting Soccer Mom Series that Charlaine Harris, *New York Times* bestselling author of the Sookie Stackhouse / True Blood series, raved "shows you what would happen if Buffy got married and kept her past a secret. It's a hoot."

Carpe Demon

California Demon

Demons Are Forever

The Demon You Know

Deja Demon

Demon Ex Machina

Pax Demonica

The Trouble with Demons

Learn more at

DemonHuntingSoccerMom.com

The Protector (Superhero) Series that *RT Book Review* magazine raves are true originals, "filled with humor, adventure and fun!"

The Cat's Fancy (prequel)

Aphrodite's Kiss

Aphrodite's Passion

Aphrodite's Secret

Aphrodite's Flame

Aphrodite's Embrace

Aphrodite's Delight

Aphrodite's Charms (boxed set)

Dead Friends and Other Dating Dilemmas

Learn more at WeProtectMortals.com

Blood Lily Chronicles

Tainted

Torn

Turned

The Blood Lily Chronicles (boxed set)

Devil May Care Series

Raising Hell

Sure As Hell

Dark Pleasures

Caress of Darkness

Find Me in Darkness

Find Me in Pleasure

Find Me in Passion

Caress of Pleasure

By J. Kenner as J.K. Beck:

Shadow Keepers Series (dark paranormal romance)

When Blood Calls

When Pleasure Rules

When Wicked Craves

When Passion Lies

When Darkness Hungers

When Temptation Burns

Shadow Keepers: Midnight

As J. Kenner:

New York Times & *USA Today* **bestselling Stark Trilogy (erotic romance)**

Release Me (a *New York Times* and *USA Today* bestseller)

Claim Me (a #2 *New York Times* bestseller!)

Complete Me (a #2 *New York Times* bestseller!)

Take Me (epilogue novella)

Tame Me (A Stark International novella)

Have Me

Say My Name

On My Knees

New York Times & *USA Today* **bestselling The Most Wanted series (erotic romance)**

Wanted

Heated

Ignited

Thanks again, and happy reading!

Love paranormal and shifters? Try out New York Times and USA Today Bestselling Author Carrie Ann Ryan's upcoming Talon Pack series.

Tattered Loyalties

Gideon shrugged out of his clothes then stepped into his shower, letting the hot water pound down his back. His muscles ached from the fight and the tension of the unknown.

He closed his eyes and spoke loudly over the hum of the water. "We're going to talk about plans to come out to the public. Or at least, plans to make plans. Then we're going to make sure our underground tunnels are in shape since the connection between the two packs is relatively new."

No one knew what would happen once the humans found out about the existence of shifters, and demons. They'd been planning for years, though, on the eventual outcome where they'd have to protect themselves from people who didn't understand and feared what they didn't know.

He let out a breath and quickly soaped up, knowing he was running late. Between the lone wolves trying to find a way to stay alive, his Pack watching him more than usual for some reason, and this meeting, he needed a damned weekend off.

He was the Alpha, however, so he knew that would never happen.

He shut off the water and got out so he could get ready for the meeting. Walker had left him alone, thankfully, and he quickly pulled on a long-sleeved cotton shirt and jeans. With any other Alpha, he'd put on something a little more formal, but this was Kade and his family—Gideon could go with a little comfort and be okay.

When he walked out to his living room to pull on his boots, he sighed. He knew they were there of course, but his wolf wasn't in the mood to deal with his entire family in one room.

"I suppose just meeting me at chambers would have been too much for all of you?"

"You love us, brother dearest," Brynn, his sister and the lone Brentwood female, teased from her perch on the edge of the couch.

Gideon pinched the bridge of his nose. "No seriously. Why are you all here?"

"Because you need us," Brandon, his youngest brother and the Talon Omega, said from the couch.

"Do I really need you here?" he asked, knowing he was fighting a lost cause.

"Of course," Max, his cousin, answered. "We're all going to the meeting anyway, why not go together?"

"We're one big happy family," Mitchell said dryly.

"What they aren't saying is that we're worried about you," Kameron, his brother and Enforcer, added in.

Gideon growled while Ryder closed his eyes and cursed.

"Really, Kameron?" Ryder put in. "I thought we had a plan."

Gideon stiffened. "A plan? Why the hell would you need a plan to deal with me? Why are you *here*?"

Brynn stood up and walked toward him. She brushed her long, dark brown hair—the same color as the rest of the Brentwoods—behind her shoulders and blinked up at him with the Brentwood blue eyes.

"You're our brother and you're hurting," she whispered. They were all wolves so they could hear her clearly. "You had to kill a lone wolf who threatened the border and wouldn't back down. Now you're having to make decisions that, as we see it, won't have an easy outcome. So, Gideon, brother mine, brother ours, we're here for you. Even if we annoy you to no end. We're here."

Gideon narrowed his eyes, even as his heart warmed at her words. Yeah, his siblings and cousins were there for him, but some things were meant for only the Alpha. If he had a mate, he'd be able to lean on her just a little, but since the goddess hadn't blessed him, he didn't have that option.

At this point, he wasn't sure he ever would.

On that depressing thought, he led his family out of his home and headed toward the meeting room. He wanted to get this over with. It wasn't like they were going to get anything done anyway. They couldn't. Not with the rest of the Packs in the US keeping silent. Parker, the Voice of the Wolves, was on a mission at the moment searching for the other Packs and trying to convince them to talk to Gideon and Kade, but Gideon didn't hold out high hopes. Parker was a Redwood, the biological son of a mass murderer, even if he'd been adopted into the Redwood family.

Some wolves just couldn't see past that, and Gideon was worried that might hurt their chances of finding a way to make all of the Packs work together. However, he could only work on one problem at a time.

They made their way as a group to the

other side of the den where the Redwoods would be entering the woods. They had to go past the sentries at the wards to be let through, but most of them had done it before. Actually, Gideon wasn't sure who Kade was bringing.

The Redwoods were in the middle of a shift in hierarchy. The younger Jamensons were taking over for their parents slowly but surely. That meant that Kade would be bringing any number of his powerhouse to the table. It didn't really matter since Gideon had met most of them and liked those he'd met. Not that he'd tell them that. No, he was still the grumpy, badass Alpha to the outside world.

It worked for him.

Kade come up first, a small smile on his face. With so many people and coming into a different den, the ceremony of walking to a meeting was a little ridiculous, and both of them knew it. It had to be done though.

Kade had brought his mate, Melanie, as well as both sets of Betas, Omegas, and

Healers with him. He'd left the Enforcers at home to protect the den with countless other wolves apparently. Interesting, but it made sense. As the younger generation came into their powers, they were learning from the older generation. It would be interesting to see how they reacted in the future when the older generation, Kade's brothers, had to step down fully.

He'd also brought his Heir, his son Finn, with him, which made sense.

He'd also brought another wolf with him. A younger woman who, from the look of her, was a Jamenson, but Gideon wasn't sure he'd ever met her. Her long chestnut brown hair flowed over her shoulders, blowing slightly in the wind. She wasn't small. No, she was at least of average height, but where most of the wolves in front of her were all muscle and strength, her body held curves and a softness he didn't see in most wolves.

Odd, he thought he'd met most, if not all the Jamensons.

Her cheekbones angled high and her plump lips thinned into a line when she looked at him. She tilted her head and blinked up at him with bright green eyes and he froze, his wolf howling.

Shocked, he almost took a step back, but it was only because of his strength as Alpha that he didn't.

Mate.

That scent, that pull on his wolf.

Mate.

"Gideon, Brentwoods," Kade said, his voice deep. "I think you've met most of us before. Probably not Brie, though. Brie, these are the Brentwoods. Brentwoods, this is Jasper and Willow's daughter, my niece, Brie."

She smiled softly, but her eyes were only on him, not on the rest of the Pack or her family. In fact, he was only looking at her, not at Kade or the others.

Holy shit.

He'd just found his mate and she was a fucking Redwood.

And from the way her wolf reached out to his, she was a submissive as well.

A Talon Alpha and a Redwood submissive?

Yeah, fate royally sucked.

Find out more in Tattered Loyalties, coming Feb 17th by Carrie Ann Ryan! You can pre-order now. The Talon Pack series is the spin off series to the Redwood Pack series which is now available. The latest release, Wicked Wolf, is part of 1,001 Dark Nights and out now!

ABOUT JULIE

Author Photo by Kathy Whittaker

A *New York Times*, *USA Today*, *Publishers Weekly*, and *Wall Street Journal* bestselling author, Julie Kenner (aka J. Kenner) writes a range of stories including romance (erotic, sexy, funny & sweet), young adult novels, chick lit suspense and paranormal mommy lit. Her foray into the latter, *Carpe Demon: Adventures of a Demon-Hunting Soccer Mom*, was selected as a Booksense Summer Paperback Pick for 2005, was a Target Breakout Book, was a Barnes & Noble Number One SFF/Fantasy bestseller for seven weeks, and is in development as a feature film with 1492 Pictures.

As J. Kenner, she also writes erotic romance (including the bestselling Stark Trilogy) as well as dark and sexy paranormal romances, including the Shadow Keeper series previously published as J.K. Beck.

You can connect with Julie through her website, www.juliekenner.com, Twitter (@juliekenner) and her Facebook pages at www.facebook.com/juliekennerbooks and www.facebook.com/jkennerbooks.

For all the news on upcoming releases, contests, and other fun stuff, be sure to sign up for her newsletter (http://eepurl.com/-tfoP).

PSIA information can be obtained at www.ICGtesting.com
inted in the USA
OW07s1804091015
7665LV00013B/179/P